THE BITCHES OF EVERAFTER

EVERAFTER BOOK ONE

BARBRA ANNINO

Dane House

For all the bitches out there. Because bitches get stuff done.

WARNING

Contains language not suitable for most princesses. May also incite belly laughs. Read in public at your own risk.

DESCRIPTION

A laugh out loud fairy tale featuring modern-day princesses with attitude.

What if one word changed your whole story?

In the mysterious town of Everafter, nothing is as it seems. Especially at Granny's dilapidated half-way house. Snow White is the newest parolee and she's determined to make the best of the situation by befriending her housemates and taking care of the property. Except the other women are guarded around Snow. And the mansion itself has secrets.

Soon, Snow gets the sense that something isn't quite right. Why do the other women seem so familiar? Are the walls whispering to her? What's on the third floor? Why are mirrors forbidden? And the biggest question of all—how did Snow end up in Everafter?

Determined to uncover the truth and find the answers to all her questions, Snow must embark on a dangerous mission to piece together the mysteries of the house—and its occupants.

Except someone is willing to kill to keep those secrets buried. And time is running out.

For more magic, sign up at www.authorbarbraannino.com.

GRIMM

PROLOGUE

You think you know these women, but you don't. They are nothing like the gentle, fearful maidens in the fairytales you have read. The faces they show to the world—bright eyes, fresh skin, cherubic cheeks—reflect not what is deep inside their hearts. Their hearts are darker than their skin, heavier than their laughter, even sharper than their tongues, and I can attest that all of them possess tongues chiseled into dagger points—one lashing by which would have a man checking that his genitals were still intact.

But it takes more than words to lead a kingdom.

Should a ruler grow too trusting or complacent in her role as princess, she just might wake up one day to discover that her story has been altered, without a trace of the original in her memoryscape. She could find herself living another life in a place that seems vaguely familiar, but isn't exactly where she belongs. Her days may seem...shadowed somehow. Her mind fragmented, as if she were trapped in a nightmare from which she will never awaken. Although the princess may not be able to put her finger directly on the mark, she knows deep inside that something is askew.

You might be wondering how I know all this. It's simple, really. I'm the one who wrote their stories. Every word, from the very first drop of ink to the last—every line, every bit of dialogue—spilled from my quill.

It might surprise you to know that I was also the one who changed their stories. Not of my own accord, of course. A scribe has not the power to alter the path of a princess, nor would I ever want to. I loathe editing. I say tell the tale once and be done with it. That's how the best work emerges. But, alas, these orders came from above my head.

The messenger who stood before my cottage door smelled of onions and rain clouds, with a pumpkin shaped head too large for his neck. He handed me a scroll which I unrolled and read. My orders were to change only one thing in each of the original five manuscripts I wrote. One *word*, really. I was to add the word "in" to the very last line—the line that concluded each of the princesses' stories. I wouldn't have to revise any other part of the books, nor would I have to add the dreaded *epilogue*. I loathe epilogues even more than editing. I say if you need to add to the story, then pen a sequel.

But for the purposes of our story, all you need to know is that once upon a time five beautiful princesses ruled the United Kingdoms of Enchantment. Five princesses who presently have no recollection of the royalty they once were, nor the harshness the world imposed on them when they were so very young.

Now, they live far, far away. In a town called Everafter.

~Jacob Grimm
    The Scribe

ONCE UPON A CRIME

"You took a wrong turn back there, Aura," Cindy said, snapping open a map that momentarily obstructed Aura's view.

The car swerved on the rocky road as Aura slapped the map away. She aimed a green-eyed glare at Cindy who smirked back, batting her long lashes.

"Well, I wasn't the one holding the map, now was I, Cindy?" Aura snapped. She blew out an impatient sigh.

The two women in the front seat of the electric silver automobile glared at each other for another brief moment. Cindy made an obscene hand gesture before reaching inside her pocket for a flask. She unscrewed the top and took a swig. Aura got a whiff of tequila.

From the back seat, a sing-song voice said, "Come on, ladies, don't fight."

The honey-haired tequila drinker and the green-eyed driver both spat, "Shut up, Snow!"

Snow balled her fists in her jacket pocket.

Next to Snow, Punzie said, "I think we should have gone to the river. I hate the canyon. It gives me the creeps. It's like an endless pit of...nothingness." She picked up her platinum braid off the floorboard and twisted it around her fingers. Punzie's security blanket (and ultimate weapon) was her hair.

Cindy moaned. "Not the fear of heights thing again." She hiccupped and downed another shot of tequila. "You swing from a pole for god's sake."

Snow said, "Doc said we aren't supposed to use the word 'fear'. It gives power to our weaknesses." Snow had been weakened long enough, for reasons she still didn't understand.

Punzie ignored Snow. "Have another drink, Cindy. Maybe you'll find a personality in the bottom of that flask." She kicked the back of Cindy's seat.

Cindy turned around to grab Punzie's braid, but the lighter-haired woman was too fast. She ducked into Snow's lap.

"Hey, maybe a personality would dry her out." Aura turned the wheel of the car she had stolen and pointed it north down Briar Patch Road toward Forest Canyon Lane.

"Up yours, Aura," Cindy said. "Don't judge me until you've walked a mile in my shoes."

"How could I do that? Didn't your ex get the shoe store in the divorce?"

Cindy huffed and turned toward her window.

Aura picked up speed, guiding the car deeper into the canyon. She flicked a look to Cindy who was still pouting. "Oh please, so your husband is gay. It happens. Get over it."

Cindy said nothing.

"Don't antagonize her, Aura," Snow said. She didn't get angry often, but this entire situation made her want to collect every animal within a sixty mile radius and take them all home for a group hug. Animals were never cruel to her—only people. She wished she could live in the forest forever just to get away from the damned human race.

"Mind your own business, Snow, and stop with the psycho-babble. We get enough of that bullshit from Doc." Punzie looked out the window at the evening sun. It was slowly slipping behind the mountain that anchored the slate colored rocks.

"Thank you, Snow," Cindy said. "At least *you* understand." She swigged some more tequila.

Aura snorted. "Of course she understands. She's..." She looked in the review mirror at the raven-haired beauty, who met her gaze with a glare. She cut her words short.

Punzie caught the exchange. "Oh, so now you're going to shut your trap? Because Snow *frowned* at you? Wow, Aura, you're getting soft."

Snow's pale skin grew even paler. She bit her tongue, but she wanted to take Punzie's braid and wrap it around her neck.

Punzie flicked Snow's cheek.

"Ouch!" Snow took her hand out of her pocket to rub the sore spot. "Don't do that again."

Punzie snorted. "Oh what are you going to do, Snow?" She gathered her hair up tighter and twisted it into a fresh knot.

Cindy said, "Well she could cut your braid off while you sleep—that's always an option. She'd probably get a medal for it, too." Cindy twisted her head to look at Punzie. "How many guys have you tried to strangle with that noose?"

"At least I wasn't dumb enough to punch a cop," Punzie said.

Cindy's face reddened with rage. "For the umpteenth time, I was aiming for my ex-husband!"

"Shut up, all of you, or I swear to God I'll pull a Thelma and Louise and drive us all into the fucking canyon!" Aura shouted.

Silence. Doctor Jack Bean had made them all watch the

movie together in a feeble attempt to force them to bond during one of their sessions. *The real strength you all have lies within you. And if you would open yourselves up to the nurturing love of female friendship, you might find that you have more in common than you think.*

The car bumped along the rocky road for a while, edging up the side of the steep cliffs, the women inside unusually quiet for a change. A lot had transpired to bring them to this moment. To bring them together. It wasn't every day a woman found herself in such dire straits. But these were no ordinary women. These were fallen women, all of whom were now inextricably bound together by one horrific thread.

None of them were happy about that.

Aura swung the car around the final curve and crested the hill. The car sputtered and struggled, so she switched it into second gear until they reached the top of the canyon where it met the evening sky. A slender woman with wavy walnut hair leaned against a large boulder tapping her foot. She was wearing faded jeans, boots, and large sunglasses despite the darkening sky.

Aura stopped the car, and the foursome stepped out.

The brunette spit out a wad of gum and said, "It's about time. Where have you bitches been?"

Aura ran her hands through her long locks. "Bella, I've had a nightmare day, so just back off, all right?"

Bella looked around at the dusty road. "You'd better not have been followed."

"Don't worry about that," Punzie said. "No one saw us. No one knows."

Bella relaxed her shoulders. "Good." She approached the group. "Let's get this over with then."

Aura walked around to the back of the car and stuck a key in the trunk. She pointed her chin at Snow. "Ready?"

Cindy parked a hand on her hip, swaying a bit. "Yeah, *Princess.*" She waved her arm over her head in an exaggerated motion. "You ready?"

Snow sighed. This had gone too far. Of course if they had cooperated with her in the first place, they may have found a solution to their dilemma before it got to this point. No one had to get hurt. Instead they fought her right from the get-go.

"It's not my fault we're in this mess," she said.

The other three began arguing about exactly who was to blame for the tangled web they found themselves in now. Aura left the trunk, heading toward the front of the car to settle the others down. With each woman trying to outdo the other by raising her voice an octave, Snow fought the urge to leave them all behind. She'd find her own way home. She could be free of them. All of them. Forever. All she had to do was run.

Except running away wasn't her style. Besides, what good would it do to leave? They were all in this together, and one way or another, they had to finish it. There was no turning back.

Finally, tired of listening to the squawking, Snow tossed up her arms. The other women were still flapping their jaws as she turned the key in the lock and the trunk popped up without a sound. Snow gasped and jumped back as if she had been burned.

It couldn't be.

And yet, it was.

She called to the others whose voices were growing louder, angrier. "Ladies?"

When no one answered she raised her voice. "Hey, guys?"

Nothing.

The thing about Snow was that she was, at heart, a gentle soul. There was a calmness in her speech, a softness to her

7

touch, a simple grace to her movements. Her very essence was a silky wave of comfort, like snuggling beneath a blanket with a favorite book in front of a glowing fire. But after spending time with these other women in court-mandated housing, a tiny nugget of her being had hardened.

She stuck two fingers in her mouth and blew out a whistle that echoed across the canyon. "I'm talking to you, bitches!"

Bella, Aura, Cindy, and Punzie all turned toward Snow, mouths agape.

They had never heard her shout, let alone swear. She took some sweet satisfaction in shocking them.

"You need to see this." She motioned for them to join her at the back of the car.

The four begrudgingly shuffled across the rocky unpaved road and toward the trunk of the car. They peered inside.

Cindy pulled out her flask and took a swig, her hand shaking. A bead of sweat formed on Aura's brow as she stood there, dumbfounded, staring at the contents of the trunk. Punzie grabbed the tequila from Cindy's quivering hand, sucked some down, and passed it to Aura who took a long pull.

Bella sighed and marched off toward her own car.

Snow stared at the person in the trunk wrapped in a rug tied with rope. Wide, flitting eyes stared back.

"Goddamnit, didn't anyone check for a pulse?" Aura muttered.

"Let's not point fingers now. It won't do any good." Snow said.

Cindy said, "The judge will add kidnapping to our crimes for sure."

"And assault. I'll have three strikes. There's no walking away from that," said Punzie.

"It's not like we can commit murder and make it all go away." Cindy hiccupped.

Bella returned with a large double-edged blade, which she flashed at the others. "Sure we can."

She leaned into the trunk.

HICKORY DICKORY DOC

E arlier that week...

DOCTOR JACK BEAN was reviewing his notes from the last anger management group session he had hosted when he heard a soft rapping on the door of his office at the Ever-after Community Center. Doctor Bean didn't like receiving patients who didn't have an appointment, nor did he particularly enjoy *any* unannounced visitors. It made him nervous when people just showed up to talk to him, and it didn't matter if it was at his office, at a coffee shop, at his home (that particular offense had resulted in more than one change of address), or, like now, at the community center where he volunteered his services. In fact, the good doctor's own mother wasn't quite sure where he presently resided, and that was just fine with him. Although, if he were candid with himself, he did wonder if perhaps he should examine this quirk (he refused to call it a phobia—

more of a coping mechanism. Phobias were fear and Jack Bean feared nothing.) Maybe he'd take it up with a colleague.

Jack cleared his throat and checked his reflection in the computer screen. He had indulged in a delicious blueberry pie and coffee with cream, no sugar, at Gretel's Cafe on Candy Lane. There was the slightest smidge of blue tucked into the dimple on his right cheek. He wiped it away, brushed his dark hair back, pasted on a smile, and opened the door.

The smile Jack usually reserved for drop-ins was tight with an air of curtness just so the person on the other side of the door was under no illusion that the intrusion was welcome. He couldn't have people thinking they could accost him at all hours of the night and day. He was a professional— he deserved respect.

However, when Dr. Bean laid his bespectacled eyes on the magnificent creature that stood before him on this warm August day, the pinched smile he had practiced so hard in the mirror fell off his face. His jawline melted, his eyes widened, and there was the tiniest flutter in his stomach.

She was several inches shorter than him, with black silky hair, skin like the cream he loved in his coffee, and lips the color of Red Delicious apples. Her scent was woodsy, yet laced with a feminine quality he couldn't pinpoint. Her eyes were bright—the brightest blue he had ever seen, like the sky just after dawn before the clouds skipped across it. A sadness etched its way around them too, and Jack resisted the urge to gather her in his arms and whisper words of reassurance. He had the uncomfortable sense that in the unlikely event a sword should appear at that moment, he would hoist it in the air and declare war against any dragon who would dare harm this exquisite woman.

Her words broke the spell. "I'm so terribly sorry to bother

you, Doctor. I was instructed to come here and speak with you."

Jack shook his head. He wanted to douse himself with cold water or deliver a slap to his own cheek. What was that nonsense? What had overcome him? He was a professional for goodness' sake. Not a schoolboy on his first date.

The curt smile returned. "I understand. Please come in." He stepped aside and the woman walked into his office.

Berries. That was the feminine scent. He leaned in to sniff her hair. She turned around and suddenly their faces were inches apart despite the height difference.

"Oh," she said, visibly startled.

Jack stepped back. "My apologies, Miss. My quarters here are rather cramped. Do sit down." He motioned to a seat across from his desk.

Her shoulders relaxed and Jack was relieved that she accepted that excuse. Better than her thinking he was a pervert. Because he wasn't.

Get it together, Jack, he chastised himself, *or it'll be you standing in front of Judge Redhood.*

Jack waited for the ebony-haired woman to sit down, then circled around to his own chair. There were three feet of desk between them now—a much safer distance.

"Now then, Miss...?"

"White. Snow White."

Even her name was breathtaking.

"Miss White. What may I help you with?"

She reached into her patchwork bag and pulled out an envelope. She flashed him a sheepish smile as she extended her arm. He noticed that her hands were slender, yet strong —her arms toned as if she chopped wood in her spare time.

He liked that.

Jack smiled and accepted the envelope. He sat back to pull out the packet of papers tucked inside. He could feel his smile fading as he read. Words like "at the bequest of the court" and "mandatory ninety days of treatment" and "crimes committed by Miss White" jumped out at him. The doctor felt dizzy. Like he'd been sucker-punched.

He looked up at this fair maiden with the eyes he'd wanted to swim in only moments ago. She couldn't possibly be a criminal. "Surely, there must be some mistake."

Snow White bowed her head. "I'm afraid there is no mistake. I am guilty as charged."

Jack sat back in his chair, studying Miss White. She didn't seem like the other lawbreakers who were ordered to attend his sessions. She was humble, shy, perhaps a little unsure of who she was as a person. But then again, he was a doctor, not a mind reader. It wasn't as if he had a stash of magic beans lying around that could immediately illuminate the character of everyone he encountered.

Jack stood. "All right, Miss White. Looks like you and I will be spending some time together. As long as you arrive promptly every week, don't do anything to violate your parole, and complete your community service, I'm sure you'll get through this difficult time and emerge an even stronger person than you are today."

Jack beamed at Snow and she lifted her head. Her lip quivered ever so slightly and for one terrifying moment, he thought she might cry. He couldn't stand to see a woman cry. It was the reason he never married. It was also the reason he became a psychologist. Jack felt that the world was full of too many people encouraging the fairer sex to be meek, weak, and submissive. He wanted to right that wrong—to change the way the world viewed females and the way females viewed themselves. His success rate had been pretty good so far. He hoped his initial assessment of Miss White, with her strong arms, and capable hands, would be another victory for humankind.

As long as she didn't cry, he was certain he could end this meeting with his reputation intact.

Jack held his breath, waiting for her to speak.

"But...don't you want to know what I did?" she asked.

Relief rushed at him. He folded the papers and tucked them into the envelope. It was the court's habit not to detail the crimes in the paperwork presented to the therapist. Personally, Jack suspected this had less to do with civil rights and more to do with Judge Redhood's twisted sense of humor. A wolf in sheep's clothing, that one. She seemed to delight in torturing Jack, and judging from the caseload he'd received this week alone she was having a ball.

"You can tell me all about it in group on Monday," Jack said. "We meet Mondays, Wednesdays, and Fridays. Nine o'clock sharp."

Her eyes widened. "In front of strangers?"

Jack nodded.

"Can't I practice first? With you?" She smiled, and a bright flash of hope floated across those crimson lips. Jack wondered if they tasted like apples.

He shook his head. "I'm sorry. House rules. Everyone shares their story at the first session. That way we're all playing on an even field."

She sat there a moment longer, her brow furrowed just a bit. Then she stood, shrugged her bag over her shoulder and turned to walk out of the office.

"See you Monday then, Miss White."

When she got to the door, she stopped. A sunray penetrated the window, creating a silhouette of her curves. Jack admired the view for a beat, grinning like a hormonal teenager.

"Doctor," she said, her back still to him. "I just want you to know..."

"Yes?" Jack asked.

She squared her shoulders and in a tone that smacked down on him like a hammer, she said, "I'm not sorry for what I did."

Snow White strolled out the door of Jack Bean's office taking with her a measure of his confidence.

TO GRANDMOTHER'S HOUSE WE GO

S now collected her small suitcase from the receptionist and stood on the steps of the community center. She checked the address she'd been given.

13 Dragon Street.

She sighed, already missing her little brick cottage in the woods with the window boxes and moonlight garden. Although Everafter could hardly qualify as a city, the hot asphalt, the cold buildings, the noisy trucks, and the tacky lampposts that lined the streets in the heart of town were offensive to her sensibilities. She longed for pine trees and oaks, moss and ivy, squirrels and rabbits. She ached for nature and the soothing sounds of birdsongs and trickling creeks. But she had made her bed. Now she had to lie in it. Hard as it might be.

She pulled out a pair of butterfly shaped sunglasses and slipped them onto her face. Then she headed south for what was to be her new home for the next three months.

It took Snow fifteen minutes to walk to the house. She was drenched with sweat by the time she arrived, and her skin felt as if fire ants were crawling all over it. She wasn't used to so much sun or heat—the temperature was much cooler in the forest, where the canopy of trees blocked the glare of the sun. She made a mental note to invest in a big floppy hat and lots of sunscreen.

She stood in front of the iron gate on the cracked sidewalk and took a deep breath, staring at the looming Victorian mansion. The wooden sign in the yard was painted with dull purple and gold letters that matched the color of the house. *Granny's Home for Girls*, it read.

Snow didn't consider herself a girl but she shrugged off the insult and stepped through the rusty gate and onto the cobblestone path.

The closer she got to the house, the more evident became its depressing state of disrepair, as if someone had given up on it long ago. The yard was freshly mowed, but the shrubs in front were being choked by weeds and brambles. The wasp nest embedded beneath a crumbling eave was better constructed than the broken gingerbread that harbored it. The porch sagged in the middle like an old woman who could no longer carry herself upright. Two dormer windows poked out from the third floor, each with a crack across its pane. They looked like tired eyes that had seen worlds of misery. The door was painted a shocking white in complete contrast with the dusty purple facade and faded gold trim, lending the entire structure a look of surprise, as if it couldn't believe the state of itself. The foundation leaned to the left side while the right tried in vain to take up the slack, knowing full well it was failing.

Once, this had been a grand home filled with love and laughter, Snow imagined. Once, the purple paint had shone, but time and her elements had chipped away at its character and pride, leaving the face of it lined with wrinkles it no longer cared to camouflage.

"You poor thing." Snow patted the warped railing.

She could have sworn she heard the house heave a weary sigh in response.

Snow shuddered and climbed the steps. She stood on the porch and pressed the buzzer.

A woman with hair the color of pink champagne and eyes like emeralds answered the door. She was wearing a white tee shirt and cut off jean shorts.

The woman's green eyes danced up and down Snow's body and suddenly she felt completely overdressed in her kitten heels and A-line skirt.

Snow was about to introduce herself when the woman shouted over her shoulder.

"Granny! We got a live one!"

She snapped her gum and blew a bubble, then opened the door wide, stepping aside to allow Snow entrance.

"Thank you," said Snow.

The woman shut the door and said, "No sweat."

She circled Snow like a shark stalking its lunch. "Nice sunglasses. Can I try them on?"

It was an odd request, but since this was likely one of her housemates Snow obliged. She set her suitcase down, removed her sunglasses and handed them to the young stranger.

The woman snatched up the shades and slid them onto her face. "Nice."

"Aura, don't even think about it!" someone shouted.

Snow looked up to where the voice had echoed from. At the top of a winding, worn staircase stood a woman no more than five feet tall. Her silver hair trailed down to her waist, met by a floral patterned skirt and nurse's shoes. She wore wire rimmed glasses and an attitude that clearly stated, *"Do not cross me."*

Aura handed the sunglasses back to Snow and rolled her eyes. "Welcome to hell in a hand basket."

She turned and called up to whom Snow assumed was Granny. "I was just trying them on. Don't get your pantyhose in a twist."

Granny slowly descended the stairs and Snow noticed she relied on the aid of a cane to help her along.

"Just keep your honey glazed hands to yourself, Missy," Granny barked.

Aura mumbled. "You help yourself to a few little items and suddenly you're a kleptomaniac."

"I wouldn't call a chop shop full of imported automobiles a 'few little items'. Now find your manners and get the blazes out of here."

Aura blew out a sigh. "Aura Rose." She did an exaggerated curtsey and rolled her eyes again.

Snow gave her a shaky smile, not sure what to make of any of this. "Snow White. A pleasure to meet you."

Aura smirked. "Give it time." She sauntered out of the room, but not before sticking her tongue out at Granny who was now at the bottom of the steps, head bent, rubbing her knees.

Snow stood there, silently hoping she didn't have to share a room with Aura and wishing she had packed a safe. With a lock.

Granny hobbled over, wincing in pain. "Damn arthritis. It acts up like a bird without a bath in this godforsaken humidity."

Snow wasn't sure what the metaphor meant, but she could see that Granny was aching. "I might be able to help you with that," Snow said. "I'm pretty handy with holistic medicine."

"What's that?" Granny scowled, her thin lips writhing like snakes.

"You know, herbs."

Granny wagged a crooked finger at Snow. "No. Don't you

bring that wacky tobacky into this house, young lady, or you'll head straight to the slammer without a hammer. You catch my mouth mojo?"

Was she speaking a different language? Snow swallowed hard. "No, that's not what I meant. I could make a salve for you to—"

"I said no," Granny snapped. "Capisce my prosciutto?"

Snow nodded, as that seemed to be the path of least destruction. "Yes, ma'am. Got it."

"That's better."

The old woman wobbled over to a large roll-top desk. The top protested as it slid into the frame. She fumbled through some papers and produced a thick long piece of cardstock. A pen hung from a chain around her sagging neck, and she used that to mark something on the card. Then she squinted at the grandfather clock that leaned against the chipped plaster wall in the large entryway. She made another note on the card and shoved it toward Snow.

The card listed the date and time, Snow's name and a number she recognized as her court case file. Before she could ask what the card was for, a slim woman with breasts the size of cantaloupes and a platinum braid that draped over the banister and down to the floor appeared at the top of the staircase.

"Granny!" she called. "Did you take my mirror again?"

She was pretty in a porn star kind of way.

"No mirrors, Punzie. You know the rules. It's not like I pulled them out of a crossword puzzle."

"How am I supposed to get ready for work without a mirror?"

The green sequined bra top and matching panties she was wearing told Snow that Punzie didn't work at the library.

"Use a hubcap, Buttercup. Now quit pestering me—can't you see I'm occupied?"

Punzie slid her eyes to Snow as if noticing her for the first time. She smiled. "Who's the stiff?"

Granny grunted.

Snow said, "Hello. I'm Snow White."

Punzie scoffed. "You're kidding."

Snow wrinkled her brow, unsure of how to respond.

Punzie stared at Snow, drinking in her tweed suitcase, patchwork bag, and tea length skirt. "Pure as the driven snow. We get all kinds here, don't we, Granny?"

Granny ignored Punzie and continued to search through her desk.

Punzie saluted Snow and said, "See you around, Princess."

Snow had purposely unbuttoned the top two buttons of her blouse after the hearing so she wouldn't come off as a goody two-shoes to her new housemates. Now she wished she had opted to remove her top altogether.

These women are going to eat me alive, she thought.

Finally, Granny found what she was looking for and handed it to Snow.

"House rules. Read them, study them, and above all, do not break them or you'll be hobblin' without a crutch. Do I make myself clear?"

Jiminy, she hoped she understood. This woman was either having a stroke or she had the strangest sense of slang Snow had ever heard. "Crystal."

"Hmm," Granny grunted and waddled down the hall and out of sight.

Good grief, what have I gotten myself into? Snow thought.

Beneath her feet, she felt the slightest vibration, as if the house was laughing at her expense.

TALKING CLOCKS AND LOLLIPOPS

S now stood in the hall for a moment wondering what she was supposed to do now. No one had bothered to tell her where her room was located, so she decided to explore a bit of her new surroundings. She shrugged her bag off her shoulder and placed it on top of the suitcase. The entryway was wide and squat with paisley print wallpaper that was peeling off at the corners. Cobwebs cluttered the unlit chandelier, and a spider was busy making his home between the dull crystals. The staircase was covered with a pale blue carpet that had seen a lot of traffic over the years. Someone had recently vacuumed it, but the stains had taken up permanent residence and were in no danger of moving out anytime soon. A needlepoint chair sat next to the door, holding a stack of yellowing, torn magazines. Snow flipped through them and pulled out a title called *The Art of Charm*. Some of the articles were "How to Properly Cross Your Legs" and "Do's and Don'ts on the First Date" and "You've Landed Your Prince, Now Keep Him."

Snow cringed at that last one, although she wasn't certain why.

The rest of the exploration would have to come later—she was exhausted. It had been a trying day and all she wanted to do was slip out of her shoes and rest. As she gathered her things, Snow thought about what she had said to the doctor and whether she still meant it.

She did. She wasn't sorry. It had been the right thing to do even if it was a crime and even if she was stuck in this creepy house with these strange women because of it.

Her eyes lifted to the winding staircase. She assumed her room was somewhere up there despite the fact that no one had indicated any such thing. Both Granny and the other woman—Punzie, was it?—had appeared from there.

The grandfather clock gonged as if taking a deep breath as Snow hoisted her suitcase up the stairs and it so startled her that she nearly toppled over.

She steadied herself, clutching the banister, and looked back at the clock with the eerie sensation that it had done that on purpose. It wasn't the top or half of any hour.

The clock face was stone still, with only the second hand ticking around it.

"Get a grip, Snow," she muttered.

At the top of the stairs was a long hallway with numbered doors along either side. There were ten rooms in all. She looked at the card Granny had given her, but found no room assignment.

Then she pulled out the house rules and saw her name scrawled across the top in a cramped cursive. Next to it was the number seven.

Seven. Why did that seem significant? Had Granny indeed told her which room she would be staying in and she had simply forgotten?

As she trudged down the hallway to the door with the brass number seven screwed into it, she wondered what she would do if it was locked. Granny hadn't given her a key.

Snow enjoyed her privacy, especially in the presence of so many women. Women didn't seem to like Snow, and she never understood why. She supposed it was because she had little in common with most of the females she had met in her life. She loved the outdoors and the woods. She liked getting her hands dirty, liked digging in the dirt, and growing her own food. Her hobbies were fishing, bird watching, kayaking, archery, and taking care of sick animals, wild or tame. She wasn't fond of fashion and didn't care for cosmetics. She wasn't interested in fame, fortune, or power like so many of the girls she had gone to school with, nor did she have much desire to date.

She liked men as much as the next girl. Men weren't complicated and they avoided drama—two traits that Snow understood. Yet she wasn't, as the article downstairs implied, looking for a prince. She was happily single and it had been her experience that many females couldn't relate to that— were frightened of it even, as if being single were contagious, or worse. They feared Snow would steal their men away. Of course nothing could be further from the truth. Snow was fiercely loyal. Betrayal simply wasn't in her nature.

Betrayal. The word echoed in her mind.

Or had someone spoken it just now? She looked over her shoulder but no one was there.

As Snow reached for the doorknob to room number seven she had the sinking sensation that someone had—or would—betray her.

But whom? And how?

"Well, Snow, there's a simple solution to that dilemma," she said to herself. "Don't let anyone get close enough."

"Do you always talk to yourself?" said a deep voice.

Snow gasped and dropped her suitcase.

She turned to meet the man behind the voice.

He had ginger hair and a crooked grin. He was only a bit

taller than Snow, with wide shoulders and biceps that his tee shirt could hardly contain. He was clean shaven and Snow could see from where she stood that a smattering of freckles covered his nose. There was a tool belt draped around the waistline of his jeans and he was holding a screwdriver.

"Sorry about that. I didn't mean to startle you." He approached her and offered the hand that wasn't holding the screwdriver.

Snow shook his hand and said, "That's all right. I wasn't expecting to hear a man's voice."

"I'm Hansel. I'm the handyman around here."

"Snow."

"The newest recruit, huh?"

"More like the newest prisoner."

Hansel smiled. "It's not so bad. Granny acts tough, but she's got a heart of gold."

"If you say so."

Hansel aimed his screwdriver at the door. "I'm here to fix the doorknob."

"Be my guest," Snow said.

"Are you sure? I can come back after you're settled."

"No, it's fine."

Hansel grinned at her again. "Great."

He opened the door and swept his arm across the threshold. "Ladies first."

Snow thanked him and picked up her suitcase.

"Let me get that for you." Hansel reached for her luggage but Snow yanked it away.

"I've got it, thanks."

Hansel furrowed his brow but didn't protest.

Snow wasn't used to opulence or large living spaces, but this room was hardly bigger than a closet. A rickety white chair stuck out from beneath a desk fashioned from an old door that had been slathered with layers of paint. Shades of blue, pink, and mint green swirled across the edges where the white top coat had chipped. It was held up by four claw-footed legs that had likely come from an old dining table. There was a bed shoved up against the far wall below a small round window. It had been stripped of its comforts, leaving not even a pillow in sight. The walls were a dull grey color, the floor warped oak planks. Next to the desk was a closet. Snow set her belongings on the floor in front of it and peeked inside. The space was only about a foot deep and two feet wide. A single wire hanger hung limply from the bar.

Snow shoved the suitcase and her bag in the closet and shut the door. She turned to find Hansel working on the doorknob, his concentration aimed at his task. A small dresser with three drawers stood opposite the closet. It had no feet and was missing a few knobs, but at least it would serve to stash her things.

Snow didn't know whether she wanted to laugh or cry. She settled on a heavy sigh and sat on the bare mattress.

Hansel looked over at her, his face open and honest. She sensed that he pitied her. She hated being pitied.

He stood abruptly and said, "You know, whenever I'm feeling blue, I find a lollipop helps." He reached into his pocket and pulled out a cherry-red sucker and held it out to Snow.

She looked at him as if he were mad.

Hansel grinned, and Snow noticed his chin had a deep dimple. He waved the candy in her face.

"It's a fact of life that you can't be sad when you're sucking on a lollipop. Give it a try."

It was so absurd that Snow couldn't resist. She accepted the sucker. "Thank you."

"There's more where that came from," he told her. "I have a bit of a sweet tooth. Although most of the other, er, residents don't eat candy. Watching their figures, I guess."

Snow managed a small smile. "I appreciate your kindness, Hansel, but I'm awfully tired."

Hansel smacked his forehead with his palm. "Of course. I'm all done here, so I'll get out of your hair. If anything else needs fixing, you just let Granny know. She'll get hold of me."

Snow thought, *my life needs fixing. Do you have a magic wand in that tool belt?* Of course she didn't dare say that. "I will. Thank you."

Hansel smiled, tucked the screwdriver into his tool belt, and headed for the door. He stopped and turned toward Snow. "You know, you seem like a nice person. Just..." he tapped the doorway with his fingers. "...remember they can't take that away from you."

Snow watched Hansel leave wondering what in the world he meant by that.

She stood up and closed the door behind the handyman. Then she pulled out Granny's house rules list and read.

G*ranny's House Rules*
    1. No alcohol
    2. No men
3. No horseplay
4. Complete all chores in a timely fashion
5. Do not be late for community service
6. Rooms must be kept tidy
7. No mirrors
8. Be on time for group therapy
9. Be on time for Sunday supper
10. No fighting
11. No foul language
12. Curfew is 9 pm
13. Stay out of areas marked "Do Not Enter"
14. Sleep in your designated room
15. Lights out by 10 pm
16. Clean the bathroom as indicated on the posted task list
17. No loud music

18. No visitors unless approved via the sign-up sheet at the designated hour

19. No books

20. Meet with your parole officer

FAILURE TO COMPLY with these rules will result in severe punishment. Three strikes will result in expulsion from Granny's house.

SNOW READ the rest of the information on the rules sheet and noted the relevant times and dates. Sunday dinner was six o'clock sharp and all the girls were to contribute in the preparation, presentation, and conversation of the meal. There would be a notice posted every Saturday night with tasks assigned to each resident.

That didn't sound so bad. Snow liked cooking, even cleaning, and she especially enjoyed making her surroundings beautiful. She looked around the dreary room that was her temporary home and wondered if she would be allowed to paint it—possibly hang some artwork or at least a curtain. Perhaps she would ask one of the other girls if that was permitted. She doubted she could make it as cozy and esthetically pleasing as her cottage, but anything was better than the depressing state of it now.

Her community service times were also noted on the sheet. Three afternoons a week at the local animal shelter. That was the best news she'd had all day. There would be no problem fulfilling those duties, she was certain. She wondered what the others had been tasked to do.

She set the sheet of paper on the desk and began to unpack. While most of the rules seemed fairly straightforward and reasonable, she couldn't help but wonder about the 'no books' and 'no mirrors' rule. She wasn't a vain woman, but it seemed odd to banish all looking glasses. And why no books? That was cruel and unusual punishment, especially with the atrocious selection of magazines in the parlor downstairs. Snow decided she would have to sneak in some reading time outside of the house. She suspected if she were to question Granny about any of her rules she would be met with hostility, and she didn't need the grief. She would do her time, keep her nose out of trouble, and get through this as painlessly as possible.

Exhausted as she was, Snow decided she should search for a linen closet so that she could make her bed and take a nap. It was the first Friday in a long while that she didn't have plans. Although now, it wouldn't be the last.

She tucked her suitcase inside the closet and went to search for bedding.

The bathroom was located at the end of the long hallway. Snow stepped inside to wash up and see if she could find sheets and blankets. The room was painted a pale pink, and someone long ago had stenciled a border of cabbage roses and vines in a circular pattern over the sink where it seemed a mirror once hung. A mirror that was no longer there. The tile and the tub were the same shade of pink, although rust stains traced the path of water from the shower head all the way down to the drain.

There was a window on the far wall and Snow peered out of it. Below, she could see the faded outline of rows where a vegetable garden must have once been. There were garlic plants trying and failing to thrive, as well as chives and dill, but it hadn't been cared for in quite some time. To her right, she spotted a lonely apple tree with a few sickly blossoms. This late in the summer, it should be hosting at least some small fruit. *What a waste of good land*, Snow thought. She imagined that Granny had grown too old or too arthritic to care for it, but she wondered why the old woman didn't enlist the help of her charges to bring the garden—and what may once have been an orchard—back to life. Surely it would cut down on expenses.

A scream pierced the bathroom door and Snow ran outside to see who owned it. It was Punzie, still wearing the green sequined top, although now with a tight black skirt over the matching bottoms. She wore platform heels taller than any Snow had ever dared and she was wrestling with what looked like a tiger.

"Beast, let go right now!"

Punzie was standing at the end of the hallway near the stairs. The animal, Snow realized, who had tiger-like stripes in black, orange, and tan, was in fact a dog. The largest dog Snow had ever laid eyes on, with a head like a watermelon, paws like dinner plates and ears that poked the ceiling.

The dog tugged on Punzie's braid, and Punzie tugged back.

"I mean it, Beast. Let. Go."

Snow stood there, her mouth agape not sure what to do. Punzie was a bit more resourceful. She removed her shoe and threw it at the dog. It bounced off him like a rubber ball.

The dog growled, still holding on to the rope that was Punzie's hair.

Snow rushed forward just as Punzie was about to remove her other shoe. "Wait, don't hurt him."

Punzie glared at her. "Do I *look* like I'm hurting him? He's about to eat my head, for fuck's sake!"

Rule number eleven. No foul language. Snow didn't want to see anyone get in trouble. "Maybe I can help."

"See if Bella's here. She's the only one that can tame Beast."

Snow didn't know who Bella was, nor where to begin looking for her, but she had a better plan of action.

She calmly walked over to the dog. Punzie was dangerously close to the edge of the stairs, and she knew if Beast let go the woman would tumble down them, especially now that she was off kilter wearing only one shoe.

"Stop pulling, Punzie. He thinks it's a game. If you give up, so will he."

Beast slid a sideways look at Snow as if she had just given away his best-kept secret.

"If I stop pulling, he's going to chew my braid off. Have you seen the size of his teeth? I can't lose my bread and butter."

Snow bent down and whispered in the dog's ear. "How about I get you a nice bone to chew on. Would you like that?"

Beast's left ear twisted sideways, aimed at Snow. She could sense his hesitation. He was considering it. "Let go of the rope and I'll get you a nice bone. And perhaps we can play fetch afterward."

Beast grunted and gave Punzie's braid another tug.

"Great plan, Princess." Punzie pulled back. "How about you let go, Beast, and I won't chop your nuts off."

"Punzie, stop pulling. I'm telling you he'll stop if you do," Snow said. To Beast she said, "I'll throw in a nice long walk too."

The dog was a tough negotiator, but that did the trick. Snow could feel Beast relenting. Unfortunately, Beast was smarter than Punzie who gave her braid one last yank just as Beast let go.

As the hazel eyed woman tumbled down the stairs, shouting obscenities the entire time, Snow was certain she saw the dog smile. He sat down.

"We'll talk about this later," she scolded Beast. He pinned his ears back and lowered his head.

Snow hurried down the stairs to see if Punzie was all right.

She reached out to help her housemate peel herself off the

floor. "Are you hurt?"

Punzie's response was, "I'm fine, no thanks to you." She examined her bruised hip as Snow rushed back up the stairs to retrieve the shoe. Beast was holding it hostage in his mouth.

"Drop." Snow said and Beast obliged.

She rushed down the stairs and handed Punzie the slobber-covered heel.

Punzie held onto the railing as she slipped the shoe on her foot, testing out her ankle. It looked swollen.

"That may be sprained," Snow said.

"It better not be or the asshole I work for will make me do lap dances all night." Punzie rubbed her shoulder where another bruise was forming. "And then I *will* cut your nuts off, Beast, you hear me?"

Beast chortled.

"I tried to help," Snow said.

Punzie sighed. "Look, Princess, I get that you're trying to fit into this house of horrors, but we all pretty much do our own thing around here. So don't make nicey-nice, don't suck up to Granny, and don't think we'll be braiding each other's hair, okay? This isn't fairytale land."

Snow put her hands up. "Fine."

Punzie grunted. Then she hobbled out the door to what Snow assumed was her job as a stripper.

After a long talk with Beast, who she discovered was Bella's dog, Snow made good on her promises. They walked, they played a few rounds of fetch with a log he found in the back yard, and afterwards she gave him a bone the size of a dinosaur leg she found in the shed near the weed-choked garden. Then Snow White, completely spent from the day's drama, fell fast asleep in a bed that still had no linens.

That night, she dreamed of a dark forest and a man brandishing a sharp ax.

ROBIN IN THE HOOD

R obin Hood used to love his job. He used to rise every morning with a smile on his face and a spring in his step because he knew that his work was important. Keeping folks who had lost their way on the straight and narrow and helping the less fortunate souls who came across his desk was a dream come true for Robin. Yes sir, being a parole officer was the life for him. He was born to do it. The satisfaction he got from turning a troubled person around and aiming him or her in the right direction was like a drug —a drug he could take every day of his life and never grow tired of. He used to walk down the street, head held high, knowing that each day he would make a difference. He was a cheerful fellow, an easy-going guy. Some even called him merry. But that all changed when Judge Redhood assigned him the case files from Granny's Home For Girls.

As he sat in his rusty Pinto in front of the rustier iron gate, Robin sipped bitter coffee from a Styrofoam cup and wondered for the umpteenth time how a man of his caliber and courage, someone who had fought against injustice in

Everafter for as long as he could remember, could wind up like this.

He cracked his neck, cringing at the pain from the shoulder injury he had sustained during his last parole meeting with Aura. She had just been about to enter the house when Robin tapped her on the shoulder. Before he knew what hit him, she had his arm twisted up behind his back and was slamming his face into the concrete.

He still had the black eye, although it was more of a yellow shade now.

The car thief insisted she hadn't known it was him. That he had startled her. That may have been true, but he couldn't help but think these women had some sort of backdoor wager in place to see who could make his life most miserable.

Robin dunked a frosted doughnut into his coffee and bit into the sugary sweetness. He never used to indulge in such confections—he viewed his body as a temple and kept in shape with fencing, running, and weight lifting. But that was twenty pounds and several bitches ago. He would never ordinarily refer to a woman in such a vulgar manner—it's just that they were so *mean*. They didn't respect Robin, the badge he stood behind, or the important work he did. They saw him as an obstacle. A man who stood in between them and their freedom. As if he wanted to catch them doing something wrong so he could add another black mark to their records. But that wasn't his intention at all.

All they had to do was stay out of trouble and Robin would be more than thrilled to sign the paperwork that would turn them loose on Everafter. They would no longer be his problem. They would be the town's problem.

So far they had *technically* kept their noses clean, but their antics and the way they taunted him were grating on his last nerve. It kept him up nights, wondering what sort of prank they might pull next, and which body part would be broken or bleeding the next day. When they might decide to tamper with his car or his computer or his cell phone. They were crafty, those women, that was for sure. Except that he could never prove it. It wasn't like he could discipline them for their smart mouths—they had the same right to speak their minds as anyone else in the eyes of the law. And injuries like the black eye he'd carried around for a week couldn't be counted against them either. If Aura swore she was only defending herself, fearing he was an ax murderer sneaking up behind her, then all he could do was take her word for it. After all, his visits were designed specifically to surprise the parolees.

The impromptu drop-ins were not Robin's idea. They were ordered by Judge Redhood, who, truth be told, wasn't very different from the women on his roster. She had a nasty streak, that one.

He took another bite of his doughnut, dreading his first meeting with this newest criminal. She looked harmless enough, with her doe eyes, modest attire, and shiny black hair, but looks, Robin had learned, could be deceiving. As an extra precaution, he was wearing a cup today. He'd learned that lesson from Punzie. She was a kicker.

He drained the rest of his coffee, tossed the cup in the back seat, and got out of the car. The Saturday morning meetings were planned. He met with all of the women as a group to collect their community service sign-offs, to ensure they had followed all of Granny's house rules, to check the therapy progress reports, and to answer any concerns they might have.

He did a quick scan of his appearance. His shirt seemed clean enough. No coffee stains this time, but it had escaped from his pants so he tucked it back in. The waistband was a bit snug. He would have to ask Marion to let the waist out again.

Sweet Marion, who was like soft rain on a summer afternoon. She was everything to Robin. She was the one thing he looked forward to every day. When he came home at night after a long day of abuse, he found comfort in Marion's arms. Often, she asked about his work, asked what troubled him, and every time he insisted it was business as usual. He didn't want to worry his bride, and more importantly he didn't want to complicate his life any more than it already was. Marion was fiercely protective of her loved ones and quick with a bow, so Robin decided it best not to tell his wife the sordid details of his latest cases, lest she take matters into her own hands.

Robin sucked in his stomach, brushed the crumbs out of his mustache, donned his cowboy hat, and approached the front door of Granny's dilapidated house, trying to appear authoritative. The one thought that ran through his mind as he pressed the buzzer was *I really need more men in my life. Maybe I should join a bowling league.*

ROSES ARE RED AND WALLS
SHOULDN'T MOVE

S now White was awakened by a flash of purple light.
She bolted upright in her tiny bed and looked out the
window that was situated next to it. Nothing but blue
skies as far as her eye could see. Strange.

She looked around her little room, disoriented at first,
wondering where she was and how she had gotten here. The
strangest feeling of *deja vu* overcame her. Then she remembered where she was and wanted to crawl back under the
covers. Except there weren't any.

She sighed, flung her legs over the side of the bed, and sat
there for a moment as her brain caught up with the rest of
her body.

After a moment, she got up to fetch her red toothbrush
and her favorite cinnamon toothpaste. She set those on the
desk along with the mint shampoo and lavender soap she
made herself, and opened the closet to decide what to wear
today. It was Saturday morning, and as far as she knew
there were chores to attend to, although she wasn't certain
what she would be tasked to do. She decided on a white tee
shirt and khaki cargo pants and laid them on the desk as

well. She had just grabbed a headband when she heard thunder. She turned, but the window was still forecasting a sunny day.

The thunder grew louder, unsteady in its rhythm, and she thought she heard a wheezing at the tail end of it. Like a freight train followed by a squeaky caboose. Only it wasn't coming from outside the *house*. The rumble was just outside the *door*.

She put her ear just above the knob Hansel had repaired yesterday, then got down on all floors to take a look through the gap where the door met the floor. Stripes. Black, tan, orange.

Beast.

"Well, at least I have one friend in this house," she said.

She guided the door open slowly, careful not to disturb the sleeping dog. His leg twitched, but his eyes remained shut and his snoring grew louder. Snow gathered her clothes and her toiletries, carefully stepped over the massive animal, and made her way to the bathroom.

She was relieved to find a lock on the bathroom door as her own room had none, although the task list mentioned on Granny's rules was nowhere in sight.

Judging from the position of the sun in the sky, Snow knew that it was still early in the morning. Five-thirty, perhaps a quarter to six. But there were a lot of other girls who needed to bathe and she had no idea if there was a time frame to begin the chores or if they were supposed to cook breakfast as a team. That in mind, she washed hurriedly, towel-dried her hair with a towel she found on a hook behind the door that had likely been used, and dressed as quickly as she could.

Snow dabbed a bit of her mint shampoo on the towel and scrubbed the shower and the sink. She wiped both spaces down, then dried them with the skirt she had slept in the night before. It was a courtesy both for the other girls and the neglected house itself.

She wrapped her dirty clothes in the towel. "I really need to find the linen closet," she muttered. "I need fresh sheets and a place to lay my head. And I can't keep using someone else's towel."

The scent of roses filled the room, and Snow lifted her eyes to find the stencil work above the sink pulsating. The green vine bulged, reached and stretched itself free of the flat wall with a popping sound. The roses writhed and fluttered, twisting until they too burst from their plaster prison. One by one, the faded blooms filled with a rich, ruby hue and transformed into living flowers parading along the green vine as if it had taken root within the wall itself. Snow smelled dirt and earth, greenery and the fragrant scent that only the most luscious of rose blossoms can deliver.

She gasped and took a step back. Her heart thumped in her chest, the blood pumping so hard she could hear it as she reached behind her back for the doorknob, not wanting to take her eyes off the spectacle that was playing out before her.

Snow stood there, her mouth agape.

Where there had been a flat surface with vines and flowers painted onto it, a cabinet had grown from the wall, framed by actual climbing roses. In that same instant one of the flowers formed its own knob.

The handle jiggled as if to say "Open me."

Snow's hands shook as she reached for the rose-shaped knob. She knew what she was seeing was simply not possible, and yet her hand was on a real flower that had somehow sprung a piece of hardware.

She had to know what was behind that wall. She held her breath and twisted.

The rose vine door swung open and there sat a pillow, a

blanket, a set of cotton sheets, and two freshly laundered towels.

Should she dare? What if this was a trick? What if Granny was testing her somehow?

But what if it wasn't? What if her eyes were playing tricks on her and this had been a linen cabinet all along?

Her hands reached in cautiously, touching the fabric. It seemed real enough, so Snow collected the linens, turned to gather her dirties and headed for the door.

She twisted the knob, then hesitated. She looked behind her where the cabinet was still open. "Thank you," she whispered. It seemed like the right thing to do, and whenever possible, Snow thought it best to do the right thing.

Fresh linens and dirty laundry in hand, she ran back to her room, where Beast was now comfortably resting on her bed, his head dangling over the side of the mattress, tongue practically licking the floor.

She shut the door and leaned against it, trembling. What had just happened? Was that real? Had she imagined it? But there was tangible proof in her hands that in fact the wall opened up and offered her the very thing she wished for.

She was cracking up. That was it. She hadn't slept well and the stress of yesterday's events had proven too much. After all, she had just spoken to a house. A *house*. Animals were one thing, sure—they were living breathing things with emotions and needs. But who talks to a house?

She wondered if she should tell Dr. Bean about this. She was only enrolled in his group sessions, but perhaps she could get some one-on-one time with him. He would surely have a logical explanation for this.

Snow blew out a sigh and pulled herself together. She put the laundry in the plastic tub in the corner of the room, and realized she had forgotten to collect her toiletries, but there was no way she was going back in there. The others could

have them. She'd just have to use the chemical-laden products they sold at the drugstore.

Beast yawned and rolled on his back, nearly toppling over
the edge of the bed.

Snow stared at the dog, a thought forming in her mind. A
theory, really. She decided to test it.

"Are you hungry?" She asked the dog. He lumbered off the
bed, his giant paws shaking the floorboards and sat in front
of her.

"Good boy. Now tell me what you'd like to eat."

Beast cocked his head and offered Snow a paw. She
shook it.

"Good boy. Now say what you want."

Beast whined and bowed his front half, his back end
sticking up in the air, tail wagging so furiously it knocked
over a lamp. He woofed once.

Snow let out a sigh of relief and ruffled the dog's ear.
"Thank Heavens you can't talk."

Maybe food was what Snow needed as well. She hadn't
eaten since yesterday morning. Perhaps after a full stomach
she would walk into that bathroom and discover there had
been a cabinet there the entire time.

She slipped out of the room, Beast at her heel, and slid
one last look back at the tiny pink bathroom.

It was just as she had left it. Door slightly ajar, light on.

Until the light clicked out.

Snow didn't look back as she raced down the steps. She
set off in search of a kitchen that she hoped wasn't stenciled
in rose vines. Or anything else for that matter.

DON'T WHISTLE WHILE YOU WORK

S now wound her way through the entrance, the parlor, a sitting room, past a few of the "Do Not Enter" doors she'd been warned about, a bookless library, and a formal dining room until she finally found the kitchen. Like the rest of the house, the kitchen had seen livelier, cleaner days. She wondered why the house seemed to be in such a shambles if chores were one of Granny's requirements for living here. The kitchen was larger than any she had ever seen and certainly bigger than her own. The entire space was painted in various shades of dingy white, either by design or because some of the surfaces had been freshened more recently than others. The counters were all constructed from butcher's block that had taken its fair share of knife wounds. The cabinets were an uninspired flat wood, glazed a darker shade than the walls, like cracked eggshells. Even the canisters on the counters, the hooks near the stove and the appliances were a drab, almost grey tone. Snow opened up a few cabinets and was not surprised to see that the dishes were colorless as well.

A back door led to the fenced yard, and Beast walked over

to it and sat down. Snow opened the door, and he trotted out to do his business.

She found coffee in the pantry and the percolator on the counter, so she got busy brewing and decided that it might be nice to make breakfast for the household. She was just reaching into the refrigerator for the eggs and cheese when she heard a loud crash from outside.

Beast barked, just once, which was all a dog of his stature needed, really.

Snow poked her head outside to find Hansel dangling from the gutter of the house, his tool belt in danger of de-pantsing him.

He looked down at Snow. "Oh, hello again."

"Hi there," Snow said, confused by his calmness.

"I trust you slept well." His feet were waving in the wind.

Snow eyed the fallen ladder. "Like a princess on a pea."

"Sorry to hear that." Hansel flashed that crooked grin. "So, any plans today?"

Snow tapped her chin with her finger. "Can't think of a one. You?"

Hansel's face glistened as he struggled to hang onto the gutter. "Oh you know, just handiwork. Speaking of which, would you mind terribly giving me a hand?"

Snow couldn't help herself. She clapped.

Above Hansel, a woman with hair the color of honey and eyes redder than a stoplight stuck her head out of a window.

"Damn it, Hansel, why must you make all that racket so bloody early in the morning! Some of us need our beauty sleep!"

"Sorry, Cindy."

Cindy let out a grunt of frustration, ignored the fact that the man was dangling three stories off the ground, and slammed her window shut.

Hansel looked down at Snow. "So about that ladder."

Snow heaved the ladder back up and angled it against the house below Hansel.

He secured his footing and looked down at her, those tender eyes full of appreciation. "Thanks a million. Sorry for the trouble."

Snow cocked her head and shielded her eyes from the glare of the sun. Why would he say that? "No trouble at all. I'm just happy you didn't fall." She gestured over her shoulder and said, "I'm making coffee. You're welcome to join me when you're done."

Hansel's eyes brightened and he seemed about to say something. Then he looked off in the distance, his head cocked, like a voice was whispering in his ear and he was straining to hear the message. His sparkling eyes dulled and a cloud passed over them. And as if the backdrop of that sunny sky behind him was all smoke and mirrors, he changed direction. "Better not. Saturdays are a bit hectic around here."

"Sure." A prickle of disappointment threaded through Snow's fair skin.

"Maybe another time," Hansel said.

"Maybe." But deep down, she doubted it. Something in her heart of hearts told her it wasn't a good idea to spend too much time with the ginger-haired gentleman. Much as she might like to.

FORTY-FIVE MINUTES LATER, there was a spinach and mushroom frittata in the oven, fresh fruit on the kitchen table, coffee in a carafe on the stove, along with plates, flatware, cups, and napkins all laid out on the counter.

Snow was whistling as she finished up the dishes when behind her, a voice said, "What the fuck do you think you're doing?"

She dropped the bowl she was scrubbing and it landed with a clatter in the sink. Snow whirled around to face Aura. The blush-toned blonde with the grabby hands had a look on her face that told Snow if she were a deer she would have already been shot.

"Are you cooking?" Aura tapped her slippered foot. Her hair was knotted and she was wearing a green tank top and polka dot pajama pants.

Snow looked back towards the stove as if the thing had somehow turned itself on. She stammered, "Well, I just thought—"

Aura interrupted her with a halting motion. "No, you didn't think, Princess. If you were thinking, you wouldn't have done something so stupid."

Why did they keep calling her Princess?

"Look, I'm just trying to be nice," Snow said, wringing a dish towel in her hands. Her face suddenly grew very hot as she heard movement behind Aura in the hallway. Was it Granny? Would she be punished?

"We don't do *nice* around here, we do what we need to do to get by. If you start cooking, Granny will get the twisted idea that we should cook and clean regularly, and before you know it she'll have us working around the clock to make this dump look like a palace and frankly, I don't have the time. Some of us have careers."

Snow chewed her lip. She was so confused. Chores were

on the rules list. Did they ignore them? Or was Granny simply lax in their enforcement?

She refrained from asking Aura what sort of retirement plan a car thief was eligible for. *So, Aura, how's your medical? Do you get dental?* But Snow was not much of a fighter and Aura looked like she had a pretty good left hook.

Thankfully, Punzie walked into the kitchen then, Cindy shuffling behind her. She was certain Aura wouldn't resort to violence with witnesses in the room. Almost.

Snow smiled at Punzie, hoping for a better reaction. "How are you feeling? Did you have a good night at work?"

Punzie balked and in a sarcastically sweet voice said, "Oh, sure it was lovely." She sank into a chair and plopped a foot on the table. That's when Snow noticed the bandage poking out of Punzie's unicorn pajama bottoms.

"Oh, no. I was afraid it might be sprained," Snow said.

"Well spank my monkey and call me a banana, Princess, you think?" Punzie leaned forward and said, a bit too loudly, "Do you know what happens to a pole dancer who can't dance? She's relegated to sit, and...I dunno...wiggle." She slapped her hands on the table. "And do you know where she has to sit?"

Snow didn't but she had a feeling the answer wasn't a recliner. She shook her head, growing more nervous with each second that ticked by.

Punzie tilted her head. "Aura, care to take a stab?"

Aura crossed her arms and looked at the ceiling. "Let's see, is it upon the lap of Mr. Slimy Steve?"

"Ding, ding, ding! Give the lady a prize." She glared at Snow. "Can you imagine what a man who goes by the very accurate nickname of Slimy Steve smells like?"

"Not good, I imagine," Snow said.

"That's right, not good." Punzie blew a stray hair from her face and curled her braid around her waist.

The timer on the oven chimed then and Snow was grateful for the distraction.

"What the fuck is that?" Punzie asked.

Cindy, who was wearing a pale blue nightie and whose head had been lolling about the table since she entered the kitchen, said, "Can you bitches please shut your pie-holes for like five seconds." Her voice sounded like she had just swallowed a good portion of the desert.

"Oh, I'm sorry, Cindy, are we keeping you up?" Aura asked.

Punzie said, "She's hung over. Again." She leaned into Cindy's ear and shouted, "Aint that right, Cin?"

House rule #1, no alcohol. How did they get away with it? Snow wondered.

Cindy lifted her head up, eyed Punzie's sprained ankle, and punched it.

Punzie screamed in agony, whipped her braid around Cindy's throat and tugged. Cindy's head slammed into the table and she cried out in pain.

"Knock it off, you guys. Granny will be up any minute and I don't want to upset her. You know what happened the last time you fought," Aura snapped.

Cindy said, "Screw you, Aura! You always take her side." Her arms flailed and she managed to get in a jab to the knee before Punzie let go.

"Oh, that is such bullshit, Cindy, and you know it. I've cleaned your gin-soaked ass up so many times, I can't even count," Aura said.

The three of them continued to bicker over the fresh fruit so Snow went to remove the eggs from the oven. She put some toast in the toaster and basically pretended that she was alone, which, given the circumstances, she sort of was.

She found a pie wedge and a knife and began slicing the

frittata into triangles. Perhaps a nutritious meal would quiet them all for a few minutes.

Snow turned back to find Aura, Cindy, and Punzie engaged in a malicious triangle that was almost as baffling to her eyes as the bathroom incident. Punzie had her braid wrapped around Aura's neck, Cindy had Punzie in a head-lock and she could only surmise that Aura was giving Cindy a wedgie.

"Breakfast," Snow called. She walked over to the table and set down the eggs and the spatula, then she went to the toaster to retrieve the toast.

It had been Snow's experience that a sit-down meal was just the thing to resolve differences between housemates. Plus, these women had a history that she had no part of and frankly wanted no stake in, so she decided that ignoring their bad behavior might be the lesser of two evils. Also, she didn't want to end up in a headlock or with her panties cinched up to her chest.

As she retrieved the butter from the refrigerator, she heard yelps. The words *Ouch!* and *Ow!* penetrated her ears. She turned to find a woman with hair the color of chestnuts and eyes to match breaking up the brawl. She wore tight dark jeans, spiky black boots, and a leather jacket. One boot rested on top of Aura's head while each of her hands held a fistful of ear. One belonged to Cindy, the other to Punzie.

Outside, Beast scratched at the door.

The woman's sly smile told Snow that this was not the first time she'd had to play referee with this group. Her agile hands sent the message that she was pretty good at it too. "I swear I can't leave you bitches alone for five minutes." Her voice was like gravel doused with kerosene. All fire and grit.

The three blondes seemed to go limp at the sound of her voice and, well, her grip. "Hey, Bella," they squeaked in unison. One by one, they let go of each other. There was straightening of clothes and muttering of "I'm sorry", and an overall feeling of calm swept through the kitchen.

Snow smiled. She was going to like Bella.

The brunette looked at the table then and frowned. "Which one of you idiots made breakfast?"

Then Cindy threw up on the frittata. All in all, not a great start to the day.

RULES ARE MEANT TO BE BROKEN

S now lifted her hand in the air, ever so slowly, just as a white mouse scurried across her foot and into the hallway. He twitched his whiskers at her and she swore the cute little thing pointed at one of the doors that read "Do Not Enter." Snow wasn't sure that she would ever get used to this house.

Bella said, "Aura, take Cindy and clean her up. Pour some coffee down her throat and wash the red out of her eyes. I'm sure the Cowboy will be here soon and we can't have him thinking she's anything less than an angel."

"Roger that." Aura stripped a curtain from its rod and tossed it over Cindy, presumably so she didn't have to touch her. The two shuffled out of the kitchen.

Bella turned to Punzie. "Try to make this place look a little less spic and span, will you?"

Punzie tossed a dish on the floor. It cracked into jagged pieces.

Bella cocked an eyebrow at her. "Really?"

Punzie regarded at the broken crockery. "Too much?"

The dark haired woman blew out a sigh. She turned on

her boot heel and waved. "New chick, come with me. We need to have a chat."

Snow didn't like the sound of that, but seeing as how Bella appeared to be the ring leader of this prickly posse, she trailed after her anyway.

The taller woman checked her watch, ducked inside one of the "Do Not Enter" rooms, and yanked Snow in after her.

She shut the door and locked it.

"We're not supposed to come in here," Snow said.

Bella pulled a string and a light shined down on them. "You're one of those, aren't you?" She planted a hand on her hip.

"One of what?" Snow asked, looking around the room. It smelled of mothballs and extinct perfume. Judging from the saddle shoes, flapper dresses, and feathered hats littering the place, she assumed this was where fashion went to die.

"A rule follower. One who doesn't understand that rules were meant to be broken."

Snow was really growing tired of the insinuating remarks that she was this innocent lamb. After what she had done, she was certainly not the purest woman to walk the earth. She had a dark side. She did. Well, maybe it was more of a dark corner, a sliver really, but still. She had sinned.

"Look, I just don't want to go to jail, all right? I would think you all would want to stay off the judge's radar for a while."

Bella smiled. "You seem smart. Smarter than a couple of those pastry puffs out there, so I'm going to make this very simple for you. The first rule of Granny's house is that there are no rules except Don't Break the Law."

Snow widened her eyes. "Seriously?"

Bella nodded, then thought for a moment. "And the Sunday dinner thing. She's a stickler for that. She says it feels like we're a family and she wants to catch up on what's going on in her girls' lives, but I suspect it's more to keep her out of the high stakes Bingo Hall. She's been clean for over five years, but she used to have a big problem with the boards if you know what I mean." Bella winked.

Snow actually had no idea what she meant, and she didn't really care, but she winked back.

Bella gave her an odd look. "All the other rules either came straight from the courts or were designed by Granny herself to make her look good."

"How so?"

Bella gestured broadly. "You think she pays for this monstrosity? No, the court does. And because of that monthly check she gets, Granny thinks that the more rules she tries to establish under her roof, the better chances she'll have of keeping the cash flowing."

"So you're saying that things like no alcohol, no foul language, lights out by ten..."

"Are all nonsense. Although honestly, she does get her Granny panties in a wad when we go into the "Do Not Enter" rooms. Most of them are locked. I have no idea why. They're only filled with junky old crap that most people throw away."

Snow considered this. Then she recalled the mirror conversation that Punzie had with Granny yesterday. "And the mirrors?"

Bella nodded. "Right. The no mirrors thing is a court mandate. I guess while we're on probation they want us to grow humble or some shit."

"No alcohol?"

"Technically, that only applies to Cindy. Ironic, isn't it?"

Snow smiled, wondering how Aura was handling her task. Which brought her to another question. "But Aura didn't want the other two fighting. She said she didn't want to upset Granny."

Bella shrugged, "Well sure, no one wants to upset Granny. We all love her. She's a pretty cool old broad. She's helped us out of a few jams and she's never narced, not once. In fact," Bella tapped her lip. "You might say she's the queen bitch around here."

Snow had no idea they felt that way, especially after the way Punzie and Aura spoke to the old woman, although now that she thought about it, if Granny were as crotchety as she tried to appear, the girls wouldn't have been as playful.

Another thought occurred to Snow. "Then why were you so concerned about getting Cindy sobered up?"

"Because the Cowboy—that's what we call our probation officer, his real name is Robin Hood—comes every Saturday at nine a.m. sharp. If he saw Cindy like that, she'd be busted for sure. Which reminds me..." She looked at her watch. "He'll be here soon."

Bella reeled off the rest of the court-imposed rules—the bits about the therapy sessions, community service hours, and curfew. She turned off the light and opened the door. "Any questions?"

Snow racked her brain but could only come up with one. "What about the books? There's none in the library."

Bella smiled like a cat with a canary in her food dish. "That's just for me. You'll find out why in group. Come on. It's time to pay the piper."

Snow turned around to shut the door behind her and she thought she saw a silvery glow emanating from the back of the closet. She pushed aside an old nurse's uniform, but all she saw was another mouse. A brown one. He winked at her and curled into a red-sequined shoe.

ROBIN'S MERRY BAND OF FEMMES

R obin Hood stood on the porch in the morning sun waiting for someone to answer the door of Granny's house. He was so jumpy about meeting the newest she-devil that he almost left his files in the car. He ran back to retrieve them and as he turned, he thought he saw a curtain flutter in an upper window. He pressed the buzzer a second time, and after a few moments he heard Granny yell, "Hold your horses!" Another cowboy reference. He hated that the girls called him that, but he supposed they would invent another nickname even if he lost the boots and the hat. Besides, he had heard them call other folks much worse. And he liked his hat. It gave him a sense of protection when he wore it, like it was a helmet shielding him from the darts they shot at him with their eyes.

Granny opened the door wearing a plaid housecoat. Her silver hair was pinned up into a tight bun, and her glasses were perched on top of it.

She squinted at him. "Who's that now?" She stood about as high as Robin's belt buckle and she was talking into it like a microphone.

"It's Robin, Granny. I'm here for the weekly check-in."

Granny's lips were sliding over her gums. It seemed she had forgotten to put her teeth in her mouth. She frowned. "Can't see a blasted thing without me spectacles."

Robin reached forward and plucked the glasses from the top of Granny's head. He placed them in her hand.

"Oh, right so." She slid them up the bridge of her nose and opened the door wider. "Come on in, I'm not air conditioning the neighborhood, you know. Coconuts don't grow on trees."

"Actually..." Robin began, and then thought better of it.

"Huh?" Granny said.

He stepped through the door and into the parlor. "Is everyone here?"

Granny scowled. "How in a dragon's eye should I know? You're here at the crack of the sun, for crying up a rope."

Robin never fully understood Granny's colloquialisms. He supposed she meant she'd just gotten up and hadn't seen the women yet.

"Go sit in the parlor," she barked. "I'll fetch them."

"We're all here, Granny."

Robin shifted his gaze to the left and there stood Bella. She was fully dressed, tapping her boot and wearing a sassy grin. Aura, Cindy, and Punzie were still in their nightclothes, while the newest member of the household, Snow White, according to the file Robin had on her, was standing off to the side looking—and this was the part that gave him pause —humble.

Not that he bought the act. This wasn't his first rodeo with these crazy clowns.

"Good, you're all here. That's a good start."

Cindy hiccupped and Punzie slapped her back. Hard.

Cindy glared at the pole dancer but she didn't retaliate.

She only said, "Thank you, Punzie. I'll be sure to return the favor someday."

"Okay ladies, let's have your sign-off sheets," Robin said.

One by one they approached Granny's desk and pulled out a manila folder. They each handed Robin a file and took a seat in the various mismatched chairs surrounding the crumbling fireplace. Except Snow White, who remained standing, hands clasped in front of her.

Robin sat down near a table and opened the file for Bella Bookless. Her community service was reading to the elderly on Monday and Wednesday afternoons and Friday evenings. Robin had had no complaints about her, and it seemed she hadn't missed a session this week. She also worked at a tavern called Witch's Brew since she lost her job at the bookstore. Her time card indicated that she hadn't missed any hours there either. Robin shuffled the papers around until he found Dr. Bean's session notes written out in his pointy, scratchy print.

Bella is progressing nicely. She seemed to have a real break-through when last we met. Her enthusiasm for her service at the Gingerbread Retirement home is refreshing. It seems she may focus her efforts on securing employment there when her probation period is complete.

Robin lifted his eyes to Bella. "So the community service is going well?"

Bella gave him a sly smile. She crossed her legs and leaned back in the thread bare green damask chair. "Absofreakin-lutely," she said.

Robin smiled. "Excellent."

"Yes sir," she said. "Those old broads really love their smut books."

Aura stifled a giggle and Robin's face flushed red. He scribbled in her file and set it aside. "Okay, Bella, you're free to go."

Bella stood up and stretched her arms. She didn't say anything as she brushed past Robin, but she did start singing a tune as she ascended the stairs. "Save a horse, ride a cowboy..."

Robin sighed. One down, four to go.

The next file he pulled was for Cindy Glass.

She must have seen her name written on the tab because she scooted her chair over to him and leaned forward, her cleavage spilling out of her negligee. She crossed her long legs, revealing flawless skin all the way up to her thigh, and caressed Robin's calf with her foot.

"How'd I do Mr. Officer?" Her voice was all silky and sweet like melted chocolate, and for a moment Robin forgot his own name.

He pushed her foot away and inched back. These seduction games were worse than the insults. They left him flustered and confused as if he had been under a spell. All in all, he preferred they just punch him the face.

He opened Cindy's file. Her session notes with the Doctor read: *Cindy is understandably still struggling with her addiction. She fights these demons every single day, but there is no evidence that she is imbibing. She seems to be getting stronger and she is coming to terms with her failed marriage.*

Judge Redhood had ordered that the punishment for Cindy's crimes would be passing out shoes from her own closet at the Everafter homeless shelter. At first, the well-off divorcée had vehemently protested the judge's sentence, but she must have come around to the idea because the reports Robin had received lately from the director were glowing, and she hadn't missed a day of duty.

"Seems everything is in order. Do you have any questions?"

"Just one." Cindy edged closer and in a husky, low voice asked, "Do you do it with your boots on?"

Robin stiffened. "You're dismissed, Cindy."

Cindy curtsied and whisked out of the room.

Robin looked around for Granny, but she always seemed to disappear during these meetings.

Next up was Aura Rose.

Aura was running the Meals on Wheels program that provided food for those who couldn't get out to shop for themselves—the disabled, the elderly, and the infirm. Her service card had also been signed off with good reviews from the customers. Her session notes from the doctor always read the same. *Aura is a highly skilled, highly talented individual. Should she remain focused on employing her gifts for good, providing for others rather than taking from them, she will definitely be an asset to Everafter and a productive member of society.*

Robin looked up to ask Aura a question, but stopped short. She was wearing his hat and grinning. He hadn't even felt her lift it from his head.

He stood and stuck his hand out.

She gave him an 'aw shucks' look. "I was just playing."

"We're done here, Aura."

"Copy that, Jack." She saluted him and skipped off into the next room.

Punzie Hightower was the next parolee Robin needed to examine. She yawned and looked at Robin accusingly. She crossed her arms and cocked her head, her braid curled up in her lap like a sleeping snake.

"What?" he said.

"You never used those free passes I gave you."

"I told you, Punzie, I'm a married man. I don't go to strip clubs."

"It's called a *gentlemen's* club. And half the losers in there are married."

Robin ignored her and checked her time sheet for work. She hadn't missed a shift. The judge had decided that working at The Fairest of Them All club was punishment enough, so rather than assign Punzie community service, she instructed the owner of the club to double the dancer's hours.

Robin wished that she had done anything but that—it only made her legs stronger. They were like tree trunks with spikes at the ends of them.

He made some notes and checked Dr. Bean's session notes. There was nothing unusual in his report, so Robin told her she could leave. She huffed off into another part of the house and Robin sat facing the last woman on his docket. Snow White.

She was still standing off to the side, biting her lower lip and shuffling her feet. There was a brown mouse just off her left shoe and it gazed at the raven haired beauty with adoration in its eyes.

He smiled at her. "Come on over here. I don't bite."

And you'd better not either, he thought.

Snow White gingerly approached him and stood with her hands still clasped. Her blue eyes brimmed with trepidation.

"Well, it seems you're the newest member of the band."

There was no file on her yet as she hadn't attended a session with Dr. Bean, nor had her community service begun.

"Yes." Her voice shook.

"How do you like the house?"

She looked around the vast room with its crumbling wallpaper and cracked ceiling. "It's fine. It could use some sprucing up, I suppose."

"Are you handy with that sort of thing? Decorating and such?"

"Yes."

"Well, I'm sure Granny would appreciate any help you could give her."

"I'm sure."

She seemed almost as meek as the mouse.

"Do you have any questions for me?"

She considered it for a moment. "None that I can think of."

Robin stood. "Granny has my card, so if you think of anything you just give me a holler. I'll be happy to help you in any way I can."

Until you do something mean like dose my tea and paint my toenails pink while I'm passed out. He was certain that Cindy had been involved with *that* disaster. It took him forever to get the polish off. Luckily, Marion wasn't home at the time.

Robin felt Snow's eyes on him as he gathered up the files. Perhaps she wouldn't be so difficult after all. She certainly didn't seem like the type to slash his tires or prank-call his phone.

Robin smiled at her and said, "Don't worry. The time will go by quickly as long as you obey the rules and stay out of trouble."

She nodded.

Robin felt good about this one. Maybe he *would* make a difference here. Although her crime was more disturbing than any of the others, she seemed truly remorseful.

As if she sensed his thoughts, Snow White said, while his hand was just about to twist the knob, "I'll stay out of trouble."

He turned back. "That's good, glad to hear it." He smiled at her.

Then she added, "But I'm not sorry. Not even a little bit." Her jaw was firm. She wasn't kidding.

Her deadly serious tone chilled Robin to the bone.

He hurried from the house of horrors, shutting the door behind him without saying another word. He started up the car, and sped away toward the judge's house.

As he drove down the block, Robin's lights flashed on, the windshield wipers swished frantically at full speed, and the radio blared country music full blast.

"Goddamn those bitches," he muttered as he eased the car up the hill to Wolf's Den Drive.

MY WHAT BIG BALLS YOU HAVE

J udge Redhood stood in her enormous home office at the end of Wolf's Den Drive, holding a bloody Mary in one hand and a golf putter in the other. She hated golf. Hated everything about the stupid sport, but her physician, Dr. Miner, thought it might help her stress levels if she developed a hobby that allowed her to relax—take her mind off her work. She told him that was what bloody Marys were for, but he seemed to think the booze would elevate her blood pressure, which was the very thing they were trying to lower, so golf it was. Except she wasn't much for the sun and wide open spaces, which was why her house was situated at the end of a pine-lined street on the edge of Sherwood Forest. So she'd had her assistant, Tink, build her an indoor course. Currently Judge Redhood, whose friends would call her Red if she had any, was on the back nine, and if not for the bloody Mary Tink had just poured she would be launching the putter right through the Tudor-style window.

She sipped the spicy drink, popped a blue cheese olive into her mouth, and said, "What's my score, Tink?"

"Perhaps you shouldn't worry so much about keeping score. Perhaps the simple joy of the game should suffice." Tink beamed her kilowatt smile at the judge, her curly turquoise hair bouncing all around her dainty shoulders. Her voice was a series of squeaks, clicks, and giggles that some people found annoying, but Judge Redhood usually found it endearing. She reminded the judge of what a dolphin or a butterfly might sound like if equipped with vocal cords.

There were a lot of things the judge didn't like besides golf—surprises, old people, infomercials, losing, soup…the list was longer than her leg. Right at the top was being questioned.

She turned to her demure assistant with the almond shaped eyes and the glittery shadow that trailed behind her wherever she walked. The judge stood up very tall, towering over Tink and said, in a voice deep and low, "What. Is. My. Score."

Tink fluttered back, her feet barely touching the ground as if she still had wings. She shuddered, then pulled out the scorecard and liberated a pencil from behind her little ear.

Judge Redhood sipped her drink, waiting for Tink to tally up the marks. She didn't like snapping at the girl. She was just a slip of a thing with a loyal streak and a dedicated work ethic, but once you allowed a subordinate to question your authority, you lost all control. And Redhood had vowed long ago that she would never again lose control.

Tink lifted her heart-shaped face up to her boss. The judge clutched her drink. Her right leg shook involuntarily like a dog's does when you rub him just right.

"Well, let's have it," said Judge Redhood.

Tink smiled broadly, although the judge thought she saw the curve of her mouth waver. "538."

The judge set her putter down and leaned against her cherry wood desk. She looked up at the ceiling and pumped her fist once. "Yes! I'm getting better." She finished her drink and smiled at the empty glass.

Tink waved her delicate arms in the air. "Yay!" She did a little cheer.

The judge stopped celebrating for a moment.

"What was my handicap, Tink?"

Tink shuffled through the pockets of her grassy colored sundress. She pulled out a notebook. "Three windows."

"That's one less than last week," the judge said with a twinge of excitement.

Tink bobbed her head up and down, grinning. "Six lamps."

"Perhaps we should install recessed lighting," Redhood said. "Make a note."

"Indeed," Tink agreed. She scribbled in her pad then checked her list. "One gardener."

"Giant Jerry?" Redhood asked, disappointment coloring her words. "Oh, no. He's the only one who can trim the trees properly. Without a ladder."

"I'm afraid so, Judge. He has two black eyes from the first hole this morning."

The judge frowned.

Tink was quick to lighten the somber mood. "It's not your fault, Judge. The upper east wing has that nasty hazard."

"Hmm," the judge said. She turned to Tink. "Perhaps we should simply do away with the entire east wing."

"But that's where I live," Tink said.

Redhood said, "Right." She lifted the glass to her lips and tapped the bottom of it, sending some ice cubes tumbling into her mouth. As she bit into the hard coldness, the judge considered the best place to relocate her assistant so that she could improve her golf game and still have the girl at her beck and call in an instant. She gazed down at Fang, her pet wolf, who was silently dozing in the corner of the room. She spun back to Tink with a fresh idea.

Before Redhood could express her thought, Tink practically shouted, "We could build a bridge between the two wings, eliminating any sharp angles. Then you could just play straight through."

Tink held her breath, her tiny body twitching.

A slow smile spread across the judge's face. She snapped her fingers and said, "There you see, Tink, that's why you and I get along so famously. You're a forward thinker, an opportunist always looking for the best solution to a problem, just like me. I like it. Get started on it right away. After you fix me one more drink. It's Saturday and I've done so well on my game I feel like indulging."

"Right away," Tink said. Then she frowned. She cocked a pointy ear toward the door. "Do you hear that?"

Judge Redhood cocked her head as well. She didn't hear a thing. Below her, Fang stirred. A low growl escaped his throat as he sat up straighter on his bed.

"It's loud, obnoxiously so," Tink said, casting a twittery glance at Fang.

Judge Redhood parted the curtains and the two women stood at the window, one straining to hear a phantom noise, the other certain that she was listening to a parade marching down the street, when Robin Hood's crappy old Pinto coasted up and parked alongside the curb. It was blinking, honking, bouncing, and blaring.

"What in all the world?" Tink asked.

The judge glanced at the clock. She hadn't realized it was so late.

"Let him in, Tink, and fix me that drink. I have a feeling there'll be a lot to celebrate today."

Tink whisked out of the room without saying another word while Judge Redhood stared out the window. A distraught, pink-faced Robin Hood exited his car, kicked the front tire, slammed the door, and trudged up the cobblestone pathway, folders in hand. He looked like a defeated man, and Red couldn't have been more pleased.

Finally! He must have something, he simply must. At least on one of them. And that was all she needed—to tear just one of those bitches away from the rest of the pack. It was the five of them all together that was the problem. She never dreamed when she came to Everafter, when she agreed to this arrangement, that they would all meet in this land, let alone be living together under the same roof. It was a nightmare, these last few weeks, as one by one they paraded through her courtroom. Not broken as she had expected, but fierce, defiant, even courageous.

If she had her way, she would have locked up the last one, Snow White, and thrown away the key. That would have solved the problem. It was Snow who the judge truly despised, not for her crimes here, but for what she had done in their homeland.

But alas, there were rules and protocol to follow. So she had to wait, had to be patient. But now time was running out. They would only grow stronger the longer they stayed together and then she didn't know what would happen. She hoped, as she watched the man she had been married to a lifetime ago—a man who only knew her now as the judge of Everafter—that he had some good news for her. From the vacant look in his eye, she supposed he did.

Redhood turned to Fang. The canine curved his neck around to look into his master's eyes, his own eyes a glowing swirl of black and gold.

The judge said softly, "Well Fang, I have a feeling you and I will be hunting in the woods and eating filet mignon for years to come. If there's one thing you can count on about a fallen princess it's that no matter how far she drops, she can always sink further."

The doorbell rang and Judge Redhood tossed her crimson locks over her shoulder, sucked down the last of her Bloody Mary, and walked behind her desk.

A LITTLE BIT OF PIXIE DUST

Generally speaking, Tink loved most things in life. She loved the wind in her hair, she loved listening to the birds sing, she loved cotton candy and cartoons, but most of all she loved freedom. There were two things she did not like. The first was working for the judge, because not only did she have no freedom, no privacy and no personal time, but she also had to deal with Fang, the second thing she didn't like. It wasn't that she didn't like dogs or house pets, it's that Fang was neither. He was a wild animal that belonged in the woods, and he seemed to sense it. However, he had a warm bed to sleep in, all the food he could eat, and his favorite toy at his disposal—Tink herself.

Every Saturday morning, Tink wrestled with the idea of slipping something into the judge's bloody Mary to make her ill so that Tink could sneak out and frolic in the sun. It was a simple fantasy, harmless, because Tink would never do such a thing for several reasons, not the least of which was that she would be the one ordered to clean up the mess.

She delivered her boss a second bloody Mary before heading to the front door to let Robin Hood in for their weekly meeting. Tink felt sorry for poor Robin, who used to be a proud, gallant man, but who seemed deflated these days. She wondered if he and the Missus were having trouble or if it had more to do with working with the judge. That was enough to shake the spring from any man's step.

Tink opened the door extra wide and smiled extra big for the man with the badge. "Hiya, Robin!"

Robin nodded. "Hey, Tink. You get cuter every time I see you, you know that?"

Tink blushed. "Thanks."

He looked toward the hall on the right where the home office was located. "Your boss in?"

Tink nodded and put a hand to the side of her mouth, shielding her lips. "She's in a pretty good mood too, so you're in luck."

"I could use some of that today, I'll tell you." Robin glanced back toward the street.

"Car trouble?" Tink asked. She had heard the thing from at least three blocks away, she was certain. Her superior hearing was her superpower.

"You could say that."

Tink shut the door behind Robin. "Come on, I'll take you to her."

They exchanged pleasantries on the way to the judge's office and Tink stopped to fluff up a ficus. When they reached the double oak doors, she knocked once. "Judge Redhood, Robin Hood is here to see you."

"Send him in," said the judge.

Tink opened the doors, and swept her hand in front of Robin. "Be my guest."

Robin thanked her, and she closed the doors behind him.

She walked a feet few down the hall until she heard the lock mechanism click. Then she shuffled back to the door, put her ear to it, and listened.

"Please have a seat, Mr. Hood. Can I have Tink bring you anything?"

Tink straightened and held her breath.

"No thank you, Judge, I'm fine."

"Now then," the judge said, "What have we got this week?"

There was some shuffling of papers. Ice clinked in a glass as the judge sipped her drink. She said, "Hm-hm. Very good."

She didn't sound like she meant it. Her voice was pinched, sour. "Snow White will begin therapy and community service this week then?"

"That's correct. As you can see, the others are doing remarkably well."

Officer Hood's voice cracked a bit at the word 'well'. Did that mean he was lying? Or was there some other meaning behind that shaky tone?

Tink pulled out her notebook and wrote down her thoughts. Her favorite thing to do in this big boring house was to eavesdrop. Not because she was nosy, but because she loved to study the human condition. She was fascinated with psychology and hoped to be a shrink someday. Not the kind that prescribed drugs, but the kind that helped people with their problems through cognitive therapy like Doctor Bean. She adored him—had a huge crush on him in fact. He told her once after one of his town hall rap sessions—his words, not Tink's—that she could intern with him, and if she liked it and did well, he'd put in a good word for her at the psychology department at the university. She had been over the moon!

Of course that was before she spoke with the judge.

"Absolutely not, Tink," the judge had said. "I need you here and fully focused on your job."

As if shoveling up dog doo the size of her head took more brains and commitment than Tink could handle.

But she needed the job and the room, and since it was all

she could ever remember doing, how else would she pay for her tuition? She had a stash saved up, so she knew someday she'd make her dream come true. Just not today.

Through the closed door, the judge said, "That's it? That's all you have?" She sounded irritated. Perhaps Tink hadn't put enough vodka in her cocktail.

Robin said, "I thought you'd be pleased. They're doing well in the program and Granny seems to have a handle on her tenants." His voice was a clipped. Robin, it seemed to Tink, didn't care for the judge's mood swings either.

The judge backpedaled. "Well, of course, I'm pleased, Robin, I'm just wondering if perhaps you aren't watching them closely enough."

"Doing my surprise rounds, just like you wanted."

Judge Redhood tapped her high-heeled foot. She didn't do that often, but Tink knew from experience that it was an anxious habit.

Why would she be anxious, Tink wondered.

A chair slid back. "I want you to up the surveillance. Watch them more closely."

"You want...I mean, what? Why?" Robin asked.

Tink bit her lip, waiting for the judge to drop the hammer on him. If there was one thing her boss didn't like, it was being questioned about anything she did or said.

To her surprise, Tink didn't hear any glass breaking or Robin being strangled with his own moustache.

Rather, she heard the false smile in the judge's words as she said, "Well isn't it obvious? I care about my town and I want only the most upstanding citizens living in it."

There was a pause. Then, "And what seems to be the trouble with your car, Officer Hood? I thought I heard a commotion before you pulled up to the house."

Hood's chair squeaked. "Electrical problem. Gotta get it looked at."

"Hmm," the judge said.

Another pause.

"If that's all, Officer Hood, you may leave now."

The chair groaned as Robin got to his feet. "I'll show myself out. See you next week."

Tink took cover behind a huge vase as Robin left the judge's office. He shut the door and turned the corner, his boots clacking along the tile. The front door opened and closed. Then Tink scurried back to the office doors.

There was silence for a moment. She heard the judge tapping on something. After a moment, Redhood said, "It's me."

There was a pause, then "I don't see how," said the judge.

Another pause. Tink had pretty good ears, but not good enough to hear across telephone wire transmissions.

"No, I don't think memory is an issue yet, but it may be soon."

What was she talking about? Whose memory?

Silence.

"I'm not certain. Could be days, could be weeks."

Another pause, longer this time. Who was on the other end of that phone call?

"My biggest concern is the treaty."

Treaty? Was she talking to some sort of government official? The mayor? The president? This was too weird.

Redhood took a deep breath, then said, "I don't think that's wise. The protocol—" She stopped abruptly.

Whoa. No one cut the judge off. Not in conversation, not on the highway, and not on the phone. Tink waited for her to explode at whomever she was speaking to. Except she didn't. She only sighed.

"No, of course not, but—"

The judge drummed her heel, faster this time. The sound vibrated through the door.

"Yes, I understand."

A long pause.

"Consider it done."

The judge hung up the phone. Tink heard a crash and the shatter of broken glass. It wouldn't be the first lamp her boss had smashed out of anger.

This was big, whatever it was. Bad too, if Judge Redhood was rattled. Tink decided then and there to pay a little more attention to what went on around this place.

For now, though, she tip-toed backwards, away from the judge's office.

She was almost near the curve in the hallway when she heard a menacing growl from behind her.

Fang.

Tink ran for her life.

SUGAR AND SPICE ISN'T ALWAYS SO NICE

I t was Saturday, and for as long as she could remember, Snow liked to do chores on Saturdays. She liked to clean, cook, bake, garden and do home repairs. She was in her room, making her bed and wondering what the consequences would be if she did just that. What if she cleaned up this place all by herself and none of the other women would have to lift a finger? Surely they wouldn't be cross with her if she took on the burden alone.

Right?

Anyway, how else was she supposed to occupy her time? She had nowhere else to be today and she knew she'd just go stir crazy sitting here twiddling her thumbs. Maybe she should speak to Granny. Certainly if Granny tasked her with something, the others couldn't be mad at Snow. And after she did begin her community service there wouldn't be enough time for chores. If she could at least give the house a proper scrub down today while she had the chance, then maybe it wouldn't sadden her so much to witness the state of it.

She decided, after fluffing up her pillow and crisping her

sheets, that she would take the gamble. Besides, she was incredibly curious about the bathroom incident. What if the linen cabinet, which seemed to appear out of nowhere, was in fact a gesture from the house itself? What if it were rewarding her somehow for caring for it? Of course deep down Snow knew there was no such thing as magic. Still, she was curious about what other secrets lay hidden inside these walls.

Snow bumped into Cindy carrying a box full of shoes on her way out of her room.

"Watch it, Princess," Cindy said. There was a cigarette dangling from her mouth and it bobbed up and down as she spoke. "These babies are worth more than this whole freaking place."

"Sorry," said Snow. "Do you need help?"

Cindy hesitated, then shrugged. "Sure, get the door."

Snow stepped around Cindy and hurried down the stairs. She opened the door just as Hansel was about to knock. They both jumped.

"Hey," said Hansel, "Didn't mean to startle you."

"That's all right," said Snow.

"I just wanted to tell Granny I was finished with the gutters. I think she may have had something else for me, so I wanted to check with her."

"Oh, certainly, come in," said Snow.

Hansel stepped through the threshold.

Cindy reached the foyer then, struggling to maintain control of both the box and her cigarette. "Hey, Hammerhead, can you get the fuck out of the way, please?"

Hansel didn't flinch at the insult. Instead he rushed to relieve the box from Cindy's arms. "Let me help you there."

Cindy relinquished the box to Hansel. She blew out a ring of smoke over his head and walked her eyes up and down his body, landing on his chiseled chest. "You know, Handy Andy, if that belt was filled with credit cards instead of rusty metal, I'd be bent over you like a gymnast on a balance beam."

Snow nearly choked. "I can't believe you said that."

Hansel's face flushed.

Cindy curved her neck, sliding her eyes to Snow. "You're adorable, aren't you?"

Snow averted her eyes. "I don't mean to be."

"Well, Princess," Cindy took a last puff and tossed the cigarette butt out the open door, "A couple of weeks with us and you won't be anymore." She tapped Snow's cheek.

Hansel grimaced. He flashed Snow an apologetic smile, which only embarrassed her further.

"Come on, Carrot-top. Those shoes aren't going to put themselves in the car. The faster I get rid of these, the faster I can torture that son of a bitch I had the misfortune of marrying by ransacking what used to be my store."

Hansel stepped out into the sunlight and Cindy followed.

Snow wondered who'd really drawn the short straw in that marriage. She also wondered if these foul-mouthed women were ever going to stop picking on her.

Emboldened by the pity she saw on Hansel's face, Snow called out, "It's Snow."

Cindy was halfway down the steps by then. She turned, shielding her eyes from the sun. "What?"

Snow faltered for just a moment like a sapling in the wind, then found a spark of courage. "My name. It isn't Princess. It's Snow. Snow White."

It took every ounce of strength she had to steady her nerves. On the inside, she was trembling, but she kept her tone even, her eyes trained on Cindy, and her jawline stern.

Cindy stared at her for the longest time, her face unreadable. Then she smiled. "Whatever you say." She turned and glided down the steps.

Snow smiled, feeling as if she had just gained a smidgen

of respect. She was proud of herself for throwing caution to the wind and speaking her mind.

Then Cindy added, "*Princess.*"

She cackled and slapped Hansel on the behind, nearly causing him to drop the box of shoes. Hansel stuck the box in the back seat of Cindy's car and shut the door. Cindy, apparently recovered from her brown-bottle flu, climbed into the driver's seat and drove away in a vehicle that cost more than Snow's cottage, waving out the window as she passed. She blew a kiss.

Even though she didn't say it aloud, Snow thought, *what a bitch.*

She sighed, keeping the door open for Hansel as he jogged back up the steps. Hansel set those impossibly golden eyes on her and said, "Don't let Cindy get to you, Snow. She's got a lot of issues to deal with right now. She's really not that bad."

Snow raised her eyebrows at him. "Is that so? Because she acts like she was raised by spider monkeys trapped in a liquor distillery."

Hansel cracked a smile. "She used to be pretty cool, actually."

"And how would you know that?" Snow asked.

Hansel stepped through the foyer and approached the staircase. "She used to be friends with my twin sister, Gretel."

So that was why Hansel was so patient with these women. He had a sister. A twin, no less.

Snow fell in step beside him.

"What do you mean 'used to be?'"

A frown wove across the handyman's face as if he regretted those last words. As if he had spilled a secret. "They don't talk as much anymore, that's all."

Something about the way he didn't make eye contact as he said that told Snow that there was far more to the story than that. So what was it? What had happened between Cindy and Gretel?

Or maybe it was just the fact that Cindy had the personality of a wild boar.

"She treats you horribly. You know that, right?" Snow asked.

They were climbing the steps that led to the upstairs rooms.

"She treats me like a big sister treats a little brother." Hansel frowned. "Well except for that last bit. Not sure what that was about. I think that might have been for your benefit."

"My benefit? Why?"

"I don't know. Marking her territory or something. She feels protective of me, I guess."

"But what does that have to do with me? I'm no threat to anyone." *Not anymore anyway.* "Certainly not to you."

They had climbed to the top of the stairs and were standing on the landing. Hansel reached for her. His hand dwarfed hers, engulfing it in his warmth, his strength. He turned to face Snow, his full lips inches from her ruby mouth. Her pulse quickened and her heart began beating so loudly that she was certain the whole house would hear it.

When he spoke, his words flowed over her like a sultry spring shower. "Oh, you're a threat, all right, Snow White. The kind of woman who inspires a man to slay a dragon, relinquish his throne, even fall on his own sword for just one kiss."

Hansel leaned in closer and Snow saw something glimmer in his eyes. An image formed. A scene, actually, of a castle poking through the sky and a man on a white horse, charging up a mountain. She blinked, and it was gone.

Hansel stepped back, breaking the spell. "Of course fraternizing with the tenants is against Granny's rules, so I wouldn't dream of such a brazen act of disobedience."

Snow felt her heart sink into her gut.

Hansel's eyes were glued to her as he said loudly, "How are you this fine afternoon, Granny?"

Snow was confused for a moment until she heard, "I don't pay you to flap your gums in the wind, boy. And you know the rules."

Hansel turned. "Aye. I knew you were there. Just having a lark."

Granny grunted. "Well, you just keep your pea shooter in your trousers and leave my girls alone. They've got enough bees in their baskets without your stinger flapping about their ears."

Snow thought it might be a benefit to everyone who entered the house if Granny came equipped with a dictionary.

Hansel walked over to Granny and kissed her cheek. "Now you know I only have eyes for you, Granny."

The old woman shoved him. "Stop that tomfoolery now, I got work for ya to do." A hint of a smile traced her lips, before they set back to that perpetual frown. She waved a piece of paper at the handyman.

Hansel grabbed it and said, "I'll get right to it."

As he passed Snow to head back downstairs, he winked and her stomach did a somersault.

Her eyes met Granny's and she thought she saw a flicker of fear pass through them. The old woman didn't speak for a moment.

"Granny? Are you all right?"

Granny stepped forward and said, "You just remember why you're here, girl. *Remember.*" She grabbed Snow's wrist and looked into her eyes.

Something about the way the old woman delivered that

last word sent a chill down Snow's spine. She nodded, not daring to speak, not knowing what Granny meant by that, and too frightened to ask.

"Hmm," Granny said.

Snow watched as Granny eased her way down the steps, her cane in one hand, a beaded purse in the other. She didn't turn her head as she opened the front door. "I'll be back soon. No shenanigans."

As the door whisked shut behind her guardian, Snow thought she heard a sigh.

Then she heard a blood-curdling scream.

SOMETIMES YOU HAVE TO KICK
A FROG

The shrieking was coming from down the hall, past the bathroom and to the left. Snow ran as fast as she could, stopping short when she saw a puff of purple smoke coming from an open doorway. She looked in to see Aura tap-dancing on her bed barefoot as if she had stepped in something vile. She was brandishing a broom and screaming her head off.

"What? What is it?" Snow looked left and right, but didn't see anything.

Aura pointed downward and said, "Kill it! Kill it!"

She tossed Snow the broom. Snow caught it and traced Aura's pointing finger to the closet where a large green frog with a swollen red nose sat staring up at her.

Snow could not believe that a woman who projected the persona of a gangster was afraid of an innocent green frog.

"I'm not going to kill it, Aura. It's a harmless little amphibian."

Aura was shaking. "It's not harmless. It tried to attack me!" She kept lifting her feet like she was trying to climb higher, except there was nowhere left to go.

Snow looked at the frog. "Is that true?"

The frog looked at Snow and blinked. Once.

"He seems to be denying the accusation."

Aura glared at Snow. "Very funny. Now kill that thing before I sick Beast on it."

Snow frowned at the frog. The frog croaked.

"Why is his nose red?"

"Because I kicked him. Then I hit him with the broom."

Snow was surprised Aura knew what a broom *was*, let alone where to find one in this house.

"Well *that* wasn't very nice."

She placed the broom outside the door and went to address the frog.

"You poor thing. I'm sorry she hit you." Snow bent down and opened her hand. The frog hopped onto it, its legs dangling over the side.

"Fine—you don't have to kill it, but get it the hell out of here," Aura said.

"Are you sure? He seems to like you. Maybe you could use a pet."

The frog swung its head toward Aura, excited by the suggestion.

"No. I do *not* need a pet. Especially one that ugly and slimy."

The frog let out a whimper.

Snow said, "I think you hurt his feelings." She petted the frog gingerly and eased closer to the bed. "Look, he won't bite you." She extended her arm.

Aura screamed again and practically leapt out the window.

"Okay, easy, Aura. Calm down."

Aura's voice trembled. "Get it out of here."

Snow almost turned around, but she stopped, an idea forming. "And what do I get in return?"

Aura glared at her. "What the hell are you talking about?"

Snow felt herself grow a bit taller. "I mean if I do this you owe me a favor."

Aura narrowed her green eyes. "You're bribing me, Princess? That's a big freaking mistake."

Snow walked over to the bed and said, "Fine." She bent to release the frog and Aura screeched, "All right, all right! What do you want?"

Snow thought about it. What she really wanted was to learn more about this house, its contents, and the strange things she felt inside of it. There was, she suspected, only one way to do that and she was certain that Aura held the key. Literally.

"I want you to help me clean."

Aura parked her hands on her hips. "Forget it." She stuck her chin out defiantly.

Snow shrugged. "Suit yourself."

She set the frog on the bed and it hopped over to Aura, looking up at her with admiration.

Aura shrieked again and jumped off the bed. "Fine, fine, I'll do it. Just..." she shot a nervous glace back to the frog. "... tell me why."

SNOW RELEASED the frog near the pond out back and rushed back upstairs to explain to Aura what she had experienced in the bathroom the day before as well as what she hoped to gain from taking care of the house. Aura stared at her as if she had grown a third limb.

"You're out of your goddamn mind, you know that?"

Snow sighed. Maybe this was a mistake, but she had come this far. There was no turning back now. "If I am, then what's the harm?"

"The harm is that you'll get yourself locked up in a looney bin and me in an adjoining cell."

"No one has to know. We don't have to tell the others. And Granny doesn't seem to notice or care one way or the other what we do with the house."

Aura looked skeptical.

Snow rushed to add, "If Granny does start to enforce chores, I'll do them. All of them."

Aura ran her hands through her hair, not entirely convinced that this was a good idea.

Snow decided to appeal to Aura's core values. She had heard once that there was honor among thieves. "You promised. A deal is a deal, right?"

Aura rolled her eyes and blew out a sigh. "Fine." She looked at the wall space where Snow had discovered the linens. It was flat now, the stencils intact. "Where do you want to start?"

"The locked rooms. Do you think you can break into them?"

A sly smile spread across Aura's young face. "Honey, give me a bobby pin and I can break into a bank vault."

"Let's go then."

Aura explained that Granny liked to go to the swap meets on Saturdays and that she shouldn't be back for hours. "But if Bella catches us, this was your idea. I don't need to get on her bad side. That bitch is crazy."

Snow thought they were all a bit nutty, but she agreed.

It took some doing, but an hour later, they had completely gone through the first forbidden room.

Aura didn't stop complaining the entire time. She whined about the smell of moth balls and rotten wood, she batted away at least six spiders and attempted to squash a mouse with her foot before Snow intervened. She coughed dramatically at the dust, griped that the room was too dark, took several bathroom breaks, and argued that Snow was slacking while she was working her fingers off taking notes.

The last complaint really got to Snow as she was hauling out an enormous spinning wheel.

"Fine. The next room, you can do all the heavy lifting and cleaning while I take inventory," Snow said as she dragged the wheel out of the closet.

Aura didn't say anything. She just stood there blinking.

Well, that shut her up, thought Snow. Except when she glanced at Aura again, she didn't see defeat or even anger on her face. She saw...wonderment.

Aura set the pen and notebook down and approached the spinning wheel, cautiously. Her stare was intense, her brow wrinkled.

"What is it?" asked Snow.

Aura didn't answer. She raised her hand toward the wheel. The closer she got to it the more bewildered she seemed. She lifted one finger ever so slightly and stretched it towards the wooden wheel. Then up towards the tip of the shiny spindle.

Suddenly, she snapped her hand back as if she had been burned. "I don't want to do this anymore."

"But you promised."

Aura shook her head, "No, I promised to open the doors. I'll give you the keys. I made a copy of the master set. You can do whatever you want, but count me out."

Panic masked her beautiful features, and she backed away from the wheel slowly, not daring to take her eyes off of it.

"Aura—"

"I said no!"

Snow watched as Aura raced away, wondering what about a spinning wheel could so spook a woman who had no qualms about grand theft auto or tampering with the wiring of a law officer's car.

She looked around at the discarded treasures of days gone past that littered the hallway. This wasn't even the largest of the rooms, and there was much more to explore. It would take forever to sort through on her own.

But she wondered, as she stared at the spindle of the wheel, if perhaps she was making a terrible mistake. A mistake that would cost them all dearly.

MIRROR, MIRROR

now couldn't understand what had upset Aura, but if
this house was going to be her home for a while, then
she wanted to get to know it inside and out. She was
careful not to make it too sparkly, too polished, because she
didn't want to upset the apple cart. She set about cleaning
with supplies she had found in the kitchen pantry by
removing a cobweb here, chasing away a family of dust
bunnies there, and making her way through the enormous
faded mansion room by room. Eventually, she came across
another "Do Not Enter" sign. It was attached to a narrow
door tucked between the library and the formal dining room.
A closet, perhaps?

She was careful to check behind her for Granny and the
other housemates. When she saw no one, she set the cleaning
products on the floor, propped the broom against the wall
and stuck keys from the set that Aura had given her into the
lock until one opened the door. It did indeed seem to be a
closet, smaller than the one Bella had pulled her into. That
one hadn't been locked and looked, for all intents and
purposes, just as one might expect a closet to look.

This room, however, completely baffled Snow.

As soon as she opened the door, a bright light greeted her, illuminating the space. The walls, shelves, floor and ceiling were all painted a stark, flat white. On top of that, numbers were scattered everywhere. Some were glued on like those you might find on a mailbox or screwed in like you might see for a house address. Others were painted or drawn on with crayon, colored markers, colored pencils, charcoal and even nail polish and lipstick. Snow noted that the numbers ranged from one to fifty-nine. Built into the walls were shelves, also white, stuffed with piles upon piles of time pieces: Digital clocks, alarm clocks, cuckoo clocks, wrist watches, pocket watches, even clocks fashioned into jewelry—necklaces, bracelets, rings. All of them were dutifully ticking away, although they didn't all keep the same time.

The noise was enough to drive anyone mad. Snow made a note in her book and shut the door.

She collected the supplies and continued past the next open room and found herself at a crossroads. Should she turn left? That would circle her around (she thought) the backside of the kitchen.

Or perhaps she should go right.

She was contemplating her decision when a bushy-tailed squirrel hopped past. He stopped, stood on his hind legs, and cocked his head. Then he disappeared down the hall and to the right.

Snow followed, wondering if she had left the door open when she put the frog out near the pond. Or perhaps someone had let Beast out and forgotten to close the door.

As the squirrel bounced across the paisley green carpet, he picked up the pace and Snow rushed to keep up with him. He made a right turn at the end of a wide, paneled corridor and Snow followed suit.

She stopped short when she came upon a second set of

stairs next to another forbidden room. She looked up. The squirrel was gone.

Snow reached into her pocket for the key ring. She tried several skeleton keys from Aura's copies, but each one failed to open the door until there were no keys left to try. *Curious*, she thought.

She climbed the stairs and found herself standing before what appeared to have once been a grand ballroom, with wide windows cut in a diamond pattern and dressed in sun-faded velvet burgundy curtains skirted with gold fringe that had lost its luster. A huge chandelier dripped from the center of the space, a grey ring above it on the ceiling as if it was missing a medallion. The crystals caught the sunbeams from the light filtering in through the windows, casting a pattern across the tapestried walls that reminded Snow of waltzing couples.

Or were they real couples? Snow whirled around, sensing she wasn't alone.

But there was no one else.

The floor was parquet, good for dancing. Snow couldn't recall the last time she had moved her feet to music, so she decided to try it out. She set the supplies tray down, kicked her shoes off and glided across the wood gracefully. She giggled to herself, feeling just a bit silly, but since there was no one around to witness her playfulness, she may as well have a little fun while she cleaned.

She got to work sweeping and dancing across the scuffed parquet, occasionally using the broom as her partner. A tune ran through her head as she moved her hips, and she hummed along to its haunting melody. She didn't quite recognize it, but somehow, somewhere, it was familiar to her. She swung the broom from side to side, skipping and dusting her way over toward the massive fireplace that anchored the far wall under a magnificent bronze stag's head.

Suddenly the fire blazed to life and Snow gasped, jumping back from the heat. The broom clattered to the floor, practically leaping from her hands. The flames formed what appeared to be an arm. Snow watched, awestruck, as the fire grew a hand, then fingers. It motioned her forward.

Come with me, the flaming fingers beckoned.

Snow stepped forward as the fire retreated back into the fireplace. A mirror, taller than she was, fizzled into place above the black marble mantle. Its gold frame was topped by a diamond-encrusted crown with a magnificent ruby heart at its center.

Snow thought it was the most gorgeous mirror she had ever seen, and yet...she felt she had seen it before. But where?

She took another step, gazing at her reflection.

In a whirl of colors and shapes like a kaleidoscope, the mirror sputtered and spun until it spit out a completely different image of Snow. She was in a cottage, only it wasn't her cottage in Everafter. It was a foreign place. Smaller, with tiny furniture and a doorway to match. This cottage seemed less homey than her festive house. She was wearing a dress she didn't recognize and a red ribbon in her hair. Then the reflection changed again as if she were watching television and someone had flipped the channel. Snow saw herself perched on an exquisite throne, her high-heeled feet barely touching the ground. Her hair was pulled back into a chignon, shielded by a tiara. Her dress was white and gold, with tiny pearls threaded throughout the strapless bodice. She was smiling at someone. A hand reached for her, but just before she accepted it, the picture flickered and changed again.

This time Snow saw herself scream as two armed men

dragged her across a tiled floor. She struggled, shouting volumeless pleas as a single tear tumbled down her cheek.

No one came to her rescue.

Snow felt her heart leap into her chest. She rubbed her eyes and tried to steady her breath.

What was that? What had she just seen?

She blinked and looked back to the mirror. It was gone, along with the fire. Snow stood there for several moments trying to make sense of what had just happened. Of what the mirror had shown her.

Remember, Granny had told her.

Was the mirror trying to tell her a story? Something about herself? Something she had forgotten? Except that wasn't Snow, not really. She had never sat on a throne. Never been dragged away by soldiers. Was it some sort of future version of herself? A costume party? Would she someday meet a prince as the magazine downstairs urged young ladies to do?

More than ever now, she knew she had to get inside all the locked rooms. This house held secrets, and whether she liked it or not—whether she even understood it—didn't matter. There was something important at the heart of all these strange experiences, and Snow was bound and determined to figure out exactly what it was. She reached inside her pocket and examined the keys Aura had given her. Why had none of them worked on the last room? What was so special about it?

She stood there in the center of that once-illustrious ballroom and jingled the keys around the ring, enjoying the clinking sound.

Then she heard something that nearly stopped her heart.

"And just what the hell do you think *you're* doing, Missy?"

EVERY ROSE HAS ITS THORN

Doctor Jack Bean enjoyed Saturday nights because on Saturday nights Gretel served turkey legs, green bean casserole, biscuits, and mashed potatoes with homemade gravy, followed by a slice of cherry pie for dessert. It was paradise on a plate for a man who'd never had a woman in his life to cook him a homemade meal. Certainly he could cook for himself, but he found the process tedious and time consuming and altogether boring when there was no one to share it with. Not that he preferred to dine in company, but the chatter in the cafe and the comforting clatter of plates and forks were a symphony that Jack enjoyed once a week. It made him feel less lonely. He relished the aromas of fresh baked bread, rich coffee, and sweet pies. And the cheery atmosphere with the brightly painted folk signs on the wall offered a welcome change of pace to his utilitarian office and his sleek condo. There was a sense of community at Gretel's and he enjoyed that. In small doses, of course.

Gretel, her brown hair pulled into a ponytail, her face free of paint, was just setting down Jack's plate of food when

Aura whisked into the restaurant looking frazzled. She made a bee line toward Jack, who averted his eyes.

If there was one thing he hated more than unannounced visitors to his office, it was unannounced patients at his dinner table. Unfortunately, Jack was a creature of habit, which meant he always sat in the same spot whenever he ate at Gretel's, and everyone knew he loved turkey legs.

Aura reached the edge of Jack's table short of breath. He had never seen her look so unkempt. She was usually cool as a cucumber.

"Doc, sorry to bother you, but can I have a minute?"

Gretel set some cutlery down next to Jack's dinner plate. She gave Aura a punchy grin. "Hey sticky fingers. Steal anything today?"

"Bite me, bitch."

"No thanks, I don't know where you've been,"

Aura ignored Gretel. "Please Doc, it's important."

"Aura, you know the Doc doesn't like to eat with company. I'll get the meals together for your deliveries and why don't you just, oh, I don't know. Go spit shine a hubcap or something?"

The rosé- blonde reared at Gretel. "How about I spit shine your face in the deep fryer, huh? How about that?"

Gretel smirked.

Aura fumed.

Jack Bean sighed. He looked longingly at the mashed potatoes and whipped butter that sat next to his homemade biscuit and said, "It's all right, Gretel. Thank you."

Gretel tossed Aura a sickeningly sweet smile, "Can I get you anything? A quart of oil perhaps?"

Aura pulled out a bill and said. "Whiskey, beer chaser."

Gretel raised an eyebrow at Doc, then took the bill and left him to his patient.

Jack wasn't certain what the protocol was in this situation, so he was relieved when Aura said, "Please, eat your dinner while I talk."

"Would you like half of my biscuit?"

She waved it away and glanced around the dining room before she spoke. Several locals took up the booths, engulfed in their own conversations.

She leaned her head forward. "Doc, is it possible to develop a fear of something suddenly? Something you never had a bad experience with? Something you never really even saw before?"

Jack cut into his turkey leg. It was moist and perfectly cooked. He looked up at Aura, considering her question. Odd, he thought. Aura had always presented herself as fearful of nothing.

"I suppose anything is possible, but it's much more likely that the fear erupted from a suppressed memory."

The turkey leg tasted as good as it looked. He spooned some mashed potatoes onto the next bite.

Gretel slapped Aura's drinks and change on the table and went away.

"A suppressed memory?" Aura's eyes brightened. "What's that?" She seemed genuinely interested in what he had to say, which was more than she ever was in group sessions.

"It's usually the result of some trauma, often from childhood. The human mind has a way of protecting itself, so should an event or an experience be so painful that it may debilitate the person, the mind can and will bury that memory deep in the psyche—Lock it away so that the person can continue to function."

Jack sipped his iced tea.

Aura bit her lip. She seemed to be struggling with something, hesitant to reveal any more. She downed her whiskey in one gulp, wiped her mouth with her sleeve and leaned forward again.

"Okay, so suppose this memory....wasn't from childhood. Suppose it seems as if it just happened yesterday, except..." Aura glanced around the dining room again.

Jack touched her arm. "Except what, Aura? What is it?"

"Except it seemed like a different version of me. Like it was me, it looked like me, it felt like me, but it wasn't me, you know?"

Jack sat back and cocked his head at Aura. "Interesting."

Aura swigged her beer. "You think I'm crazy."

"No, not at all. Were you sleeping? Could it have been a dream?"

"No. Wide awake."

The doctor sat silent for a time. "Perhaps what you experienced was a vision. A manifestation of the thing you fear."

Aura ran her hands through her hair. "No, I don't think so. Because this...object. I've only seen one like it before at the home of one of the Meals on Wheels clients. She...wanted to give it to me, but I wasn't afraid then."

Jack rolled her words over in his mind and was careful to choose his response wisely before he spoke again. He set his fork down. "The human mind is still a vast mystery to science, Aura. It is capable of things we cannot even imagine."

Aura nodded.

Jack leaned closer. "Is it possible that you unconsciously stole this object and now you feel remorse?"

Aura's jaw dropped. "What? No. How could you ask me such a thing?"

"Aura, I'm just trying to help." Jack patted her wrist. "Sometimes we regress, and impulses we thought we left behind us resurface again. We're human, after all. We make mistakes."

Her voice rose and heads began to swing their way. "You don't seem real human right now, Doc. In fact, you seem like an arrogant asshole who just shit on someone who came to him for help."

"Now, Aura, listen—"

"No. You're accusing me just like everyone else." She stood up, pointed a finger at Jack. "You listen to me, *Doctor*. I've served my time and I've changed whether or not you believe it." She swept her arm across the diner. "And I really don't give a flying monkey fuck if any of you believe me. I know the truth." Her voice broke and for a frightening moment Jack thought she might cry.

Jack sat there stunned. Not just at her behavior, but at his own accusation. For the first time in his life, he didn't know what to say.

Aura stood, poured the remainder of her beer over Jack's dinner and said, "*Bon Appétit.*"

Her hips swayed as she walked to the door. She grabbed the bag of boxed dinners off the counter near the register and put her hand on the shiny stainless steel handle of the entrance. She stopped, turned and said, "Oh and just FYI, Doc, I know where you live."

Jack felt his stomach twist into a knot. He hoped he wouldn't have to move again.

Aura swung the door open just as Robin Hood entered the cafe. She pinched him on the cheek and walked out.

Across the restaurant at the counter, Tink twirled around in her stool and waved at Jack.

BELLA OF THE BALL

S now spun around, the keys jingling in her hand, to find Bella standing in the open doorway arms crossed, one eyebrow strategically arched, tapping her black leather boot on the parquet floor. Snow slid her eyes around the ballroom as if an answer to Bella's question would appear out of thin air.

Bella walked toward Snow, her heels thumping on the floor. She picked up the broom and held it out to Snow. "I thought we had an agreement. Remember?" She pointed at Snow and in a thick, stilted voice said, "You no cleany. Cleany bad. Make work for all."

Snow just blinked at her, stone still.

Bella sighed and dropped the broom. It landed with a smacking sound. "That was my impersonation of a giant. Most people laugh."

Of course it was. Why was she so on edge around these women? Snow tossed her head back and cackled. "I'm sorry, I thought maybe you were having a stroke." She slapped her knee. "That was a good one, Bella. Very amusing."

The brunette wrinkled her nose at Snow and brushed

past her. She circled the room, sniffing the air. "Did you light a fire? It smells of burning embers in here."

She approached the fireplace and crouched down to take a better look. Steadying herself, she placed a hand on one knee for balance, grabbed a poker and prodded the bricks.

There was no trace of ash from the phantom fire, and Snow was grateful. She had enough to worry about with Aura, this mysterious house, and whatever might be in that locked room without humiliating herself in front of the only woman she respected here.

Bella had good sense. She radiated awareness, intelligence, and a longing to *know things*, which probably made the no-books rule all that much more frustrating. On a few occasions Snow had spotted Bella flipping through discarded newspapers, reading instruction manuals, even skimming the backs of cereal boxes, shampoo bottles, and warning labels. Snow wondered why that rule had been implemented at all. What had Bella done to deserve such a harsh punishment?

The silence had spread throughout the room and Snow thought she should fill it with an explanation. "I'm sorry Bella, but with Granny's bad leg, I didn't see the harm in tidying up here on the second floor."

Bella aimed her gaze at Snow. "Really? So who cleaned up the rest of the place then? Forest creatures?"

Bella was still exploring the ballroom. She reached over and touched a curtain, staring out the window for the longest time. She seemed mesmerized by something—or someone—outside. Frozen in place.

Snow crept forward, her keys clinking. "Bella, are you all right?"

She didn't answer.

The window was steps away, so Snow took a look for

herself. All she saw was Beast lying in the grass, soaking up the sun, and Hansel, mowing the lawn, shirtless.

Bella shook her head. "Yes, I'm fine." She seemed to break away from the temporary trance. She turned to gape at the room once more. "I've never been up here. I thought I heard a noise, so I followed it. I never even knew those back stairs existed." Her face screwed into a mask of wonder and her head tilted as though she were listening to a song that stopped playing long ago. "It's strange...it...feels familiar to me." Her voice was soft, a whisper almost.

Snow widened her eyes. Did Bella feel it too? Was something happening to her as well? "It does? How so?"

"I don't know. It's the curtains." She waved her hand toward them. "Or maybe the fireplace, or—" She stopped short, as if she were about to reveal something she wanted no one to ever know. Something that would cause her a great deal of pain.

Her tone brightened as she sprung over to the fireplace. "Or maybe there's a magical linen closet hidden behind that wall." She looked at Snow and added, "Muahhhahahahhah." Her eyes bulged as she mimicked Frankenstein.

Snow crossed her arms. "Very funny." She knew these women were feeling the same things she was even if they didn't *see* the same things. Although she was certain both Aura in the closet and now Bella at the window had seen or felt something. So why wouldn't they admit to it?

Bella said, "I couldn't resist. I ran into Aura on her way out. She told me about your little "episode." She drew air quotes.

Snow cast a hard look, whirled around, picked up the broom, and walked away from Bella.

Bella followed Snow down the stairs. "Hey don't run away pissed off."

Snow smirked. "Just run away, right? Another zinger, Bella."

"Hold on, I wasn't going to say that. My jokes are much more advanced."

Snow hurried down the stairs. What was the point anyway? She knew these people didn't like her, and she didn't really care all that much for them. It was just that they shared this one horrible experience in common and weren't people supposed to bond over things like that?

"Can you slow down, please?"

"Forget it, Bella."

They reached the end of the stairwell. Bella grabbed the neck of Snow White's shirt and yanked her backward. She spun her around, shoved her down onto the last step and said, "You need to calm down."

"I'm perfectly calm."

Bella said, "You're not going to last if you don't learn to take a joke once in a while. Or a punch."

Snow frowned, touching her cheek. She hadn't ever been struck before and she wasn't convinced she could take a blow.

Bella tapped Snow's knee with her foot. "I was kidding about the punch. But just in case, stay away from Cindy when she's hammered." Bella thought for a moment, tapping her chin. "And Punzie, just in general."

Bella cracked a smile and Snow couldn't help but match it. She stood and pulled out the key ring Aura had given her. She motioned over to the door she wasn't able to unlock earlier. "None of the keys fit this one."

A slow smile spread across Bella's face. "Well, I'll be damned, Princess. You've got a bit of dark blood in you after all." She parked her hands on her hips. "How in the hell did you pry those from that greedy bitch's hands?"

Snow twirled the key ring feeling a bit brazen. "I helped her with an infestation problem."

Bella clapped her hands. "Ha! You bribed her? I love it." Her face got serious. "Bugs?"

"Frog. Singular."

Bella shook her head. "Is that the one that's been stalking Punzie around the house? She told me she was going to catch it and put it in Aura's room. I just didn't think she had the gonads to do it."

Snow shrugged. "I guess so." She twirled the keys in her hand. "None of these unlock that door. Do you know what's in there?"

"Your guess is as good as mine. It's always been locked. Some of them, like that closet we snuck into yesterday, are never locked. There's no rhyme or reason around here."

Snow wondered if Aura really could break into anything. Maybe if she had the right motivation.

Bella said, "You know it's just junk in these rooms. Granny's a flea market, garage sale, swap meet, auction house addict. To her it's a safer form of gambling. She buys all this junk, tosses it into these dusty old rooms and forgets about it. You really are wasting your time. There's no holy grail in this house."

But what about the clocks? Surely that collection, tucked away as it was, had to signify something. Didn't it? Snow decided not to mention it to Bella. At least not until she had more time to figure this place out.

Bella said, "Look it's getting late and Granny will be coming home soon. Don't let her catch you with those keys and especially not the cleaning supplies. Got it?"

"Got it."

Bella nodded and started away.

After a moment, Snow said, "Bella?"

She turned. "Yes?"

"Thank you."

"For what?"

"For being my friend."

Bella stared at Snow a few beats, a gloomy expression clouding her face. "We're not friends, Princess. This isn't a fairy tale."

Snow stiffened. Every time she thought she was making strides to fit in, she got sucker-punched. "What are we then?" she asked in a tight-lipped voice. She hoped she sounded mean. She wanted to be mean back, just once.

Bella spread her arms wide and smiled. "Partners in crime, of course."

Snow flipped the keys in her hand, watching Bella saunter down the hall and wondered.

Would she be able to commit another crime? If it meant finding out the truth?

DON'T PISS OFF THE PIXIE

The only free time Tink had was a few hours on Saturday nights, and she used every bit of it to get closer to Doctor Jack Bean. Except this night. That kook, Aura, had ruined her plans by causing a scene and spoiling the good doctor's meal. He went home early, a grim look on his face, before Tink could even say a proper hello.

Stupid Aura with her stupid temper and her stupid anger management sessions where she gets to see the doctor three days a week, Tink thought as she drove back to the judge's house. And for what? Because she broke the law, she got to spend time in the presence of that great man.

Well Tink thought that was absurd. She had a good mind to break the law herself if she thought it wouldn't get her fired. Then she could see more of the doctor too.

Tink realized she'd been lost in her anger when she saw Aura's strawberry blonde hair flapping out of the car window in front of her.

She thought back to the meeting she had overheard between Robin Hood and the judge and an idea formed in her mind—an idea that ordinarily would never occur to a soul as sweet as Tink's, but love and rage had blinded her.

She pressed her foot more firmly on the gas pedal, barely making the green arrow for her left turn. There was Aura still ahead of her. Tink was close enough to follow, yet far enough away not to be spotted. She was pretty sure that's how they did it in spy novels. Tink was a huge fan of John Rain books.

What was it the judge had said to Robin? Something about keeping closer tabs on the girls at Granny's? Upping the surveillance. He hadn't seemed too pleased about that suggestion as she recalled. In fact, he seemed downright put out. But when one of these wretched women hurts a man as gallant as Jack Bean, well then she should be watched with a closer eye. Luckily, Tink's eyes were as sharp as her ears.

The car Aura was driving made another left and pulled into a quiet driveway on a dark street in front of a brick ranch home. Tink watched as Aura got out of the car and retrieved something from the back seat. It was a bag of food from Gretel's. Part of Aura's punishment was to volunteer for meals on wheels, so perhaps that was what she was doing now.

Aura rang the bell and a gray haired woman answered. They spoke to each other briefly, the woman sticking her hand out of the door to motion for Aura to enter. Aura stepped inside and the door closed behind her.

"I've got my eye on you, Aura Rose," Tink said.

Perhaps, if all went well and she was able to find that Aura had broken the law or violated probation, the judge might give Tink a raise.

If that didn't work, there was always plan B.

ROBIN HOOD RARELY GOT ANGRY, but when he did he drank milk straight from the bottle and ate a double cheeseburger with everything on it. He was a wild man tonight.

He was already wolfing down his second double cheese-burger and had nearly finished the entire quart of milk, and it wasn't even eight o'clock. Robin had earmarked both of these items to bring home to his bride. And he would have except that insufferable judge had sent her assistant, Tink, to do Robin's job.

This should have been an easy run. Make sure Aura was where she was supposed to be. She is. The end.

But here he had a civilian running her own stakeout. Aura was taking longer than she should on her delivery, and there was no bathroom in sight. Any minute now, Robin would be forced to finish the milk and deposit it right back into the bottle.

So much for date night with the wife. The greasy burger would have been a bad enough substitute for a romantic dinner, but at least it would have told Marion he had been thinking about her. Now what was he supposed to bring her? Certainly not the milk jug.

Robin was contemplating what stores were open on his route home when a bright flash of light exploded from the house followed by a booming noise. Everything on the block fell into darkness. There wasn't a street lamp, porch light, or night light lit on the entire street.

"What the heck?"

Robin tried to start his own car, to no avail. "Aw, damn, not again!" He slammed his fist on the steering wheel.

There was a wave of movement to his right. He looked over and saw that Aura's car was gone.

Except it hadn't made a sound. It had simply vanished.

Tink's car was parked in the same spot as when Robin had pulled up. She got out, checked under the hood, then threw her hands in the air in frustration.

Robin was debating his next move when the streetlights flickered and Tink stood there staring at Robin like a deer caught in headlights.

FORBIDDEN FRUIT

S now wasn't looking forward to Sunday night dinner. For one thing, it was clear that she had no friends in this house except for Cotton, the white mouse, and Peanut, the brown mouse, who seemed to have an uncanny knack for showing up just when she needed them. She fashioned them each a small bed from tissue and cotton balls and tucked them away inside the desk drawer where they slumbered softly throughout the night. There was Beast, of course, but he was much more drawn to Bella, so Snow benefited from his slobbery company mostly when Bella was out. She didn't mind that, as Bella needed the softness that only an animal can bring, but it did get rather lonely.

Hansel had been nothing but sweet to her, but Snow thought it was best not to tempt fate by breaking Granny's rules. She didn't want to be reprimanded by the court or the old woman, and she certainly didn't want Hansel to lose his job over her.

There was also the small matter of the walls whispering the word *betrayal* to her every so often. She never matched a face with the voice, and sometimes she felt that it wasn't from an outside source at all, but that it came right from her own head. She didn't know what it meant or who it was referring to, but she figured that keeping the rest of the housemates at elbow's length wasn't the worst idea.

Maybe deep in the recesses of their minds they heard it too. Maybe that's why everyone was so callous.

Snow was unloading the groceries for tonight's feast when Punzie sashayed into the kitchen wearing leggings, flip flops, and a roomy tee shirt with a crooked crown printed on the front and the words "I'm the Fairest" splashed across the back in bold pink letters.

Behind her hopped a frog.

Snow stared at the frog, whose nose was still a violent red where Aura had kicked it.

Punzie said, "I'm starving, when's dinner?" She poked her head through a couple of the bags and pulled out a vine of grapes.

"When is it usually?" Snow asked. She began unloading the vegetables she had purchased at the farmer's market for the salad.

Punzie said, "I think seven. Sundays are my only day off, so I don't pay too much attention to the clock."

Snow was confused. "But don't you usually all cook together?"

Punzie smirked. "Us cook? Are you serious?" Punzie washed the grapes in the sink and set them in the bowl. She offered one to the frog. It declined, catching a fly in mid-flight instead.

"We usually order from Gretel's and Hansel picks it up." She winked and elbowed Snow. "What Granny doesn't know won't hurt her. All she cares about is that we're all here for the meal anyway."

The frog made a *ribbet* sound and Snow said, "Will your green friend be joining us?" She put the tomatoes, cucumber, carrots, and lettuce in a large colander and set it in the sink.

Punzie frowned. "This thing won't leave me alone, but I feel kind of sorry for it."

Snow perked up at this. "Why?" She turned the water on and sprayed down the vegetables.

The dancer shrugged. "I don't know. But I get the feeling he lost his mate or something."

Snow shut the water off and turned to look at the frog. Both women stood side by side trying to decipher the emotional needs of a slick-backed amphibian.

Punzie said, "You see how he keeps staring at my boobs? I think he's horny."

"I thought that was toads."

Punzie shifted her gaze to Snow. "Well slap my ass, the Princess just told a dirty joke."

Snow rolled her eyes and went back to shaking the excess water out of her produce.

Punzie said, "Well, call me when dinner's ready. Bob and I are going down to the pond to pick up chicks."

Snow spun toward the back door that Punzie was about to walk through, the frog close at her heels. "You're not going to help me?"

Punzie had her hand on the screen door. She turned back to Snow. "Why do you need my help? I thought you loved this shit."

Snow looked at the bags of groceries spread across the kitchen. She hadn't cooked for a crowd in, in, well she couldn't remember when the last time was, but she was sure she had a little help. "Well, yes, but, I mean—"

"Great! Catch ya later. Come on, Bob."

Punzie slapped the screen door open and Bob hopped outside.

"Catch ya later," Snow mimicked Punzie's high pitch and added a snotty twang to it. She made a face at the door.

"I guess the answer is yes."

Snow jumped at the sound of the voice and turned to see Hansel's rugged face gazing at her. He was wearing a crisp white shirt that highlighted his tan, dark blue jeans, and a high voltage smile. His hair was slightly damp as if he'd recently showered. He smelled like the forest on an autumn morning. It reminded Snow of home, and she wanted to crawl between his arms and get lost there.

"The answer to what?"

Hansel gave her head a playful tap. "You *do* talk to yourself a lot."

Snow smoothed a stray black hair away from her face and patted down her apron. "Oh that. Well, I suppose that's true mostly because no one else talks to me around here unless they want something or they want something to bitch about or, you know, they need a punching bag."

The groceries weren't going to unpack themselves, Snow told herself. She also chastised herself for looking like a fool every time this man was around. Good grief, why did he always have to sneak up on her like that?

Hansel tilted his head. "Are you okay?"

"I'm fine." She yanked the potatoes from the bag and dropped them on the kitchen table.

"You sure?" Hansel asked. "Because you don't seem fine."

Snow could feel a well bubbling up inside her, but the last thing she wanted was for Hansel—or anyone in this house for that matter—to see her shed a single tear.

She gritted her teeth, still unloading the groceries, and carefully avoided Hansel's golden eyes. "What do you want, Hansel?"

He didn't answer her for a few seconds and Snow could feel him staring at her. Likely sizing up what size straight jacket might suit her best. "I'm here to take your dinner order. It's Sunday."

"Yes, well, I'm cooking. There will be no take-out this evening, thank you."

She brushed past him to put the sugar, vanilla, and flour on the counter. She was going to make a pie for dessert.

"Oh, okay then." Hansel seemed nailed to his spot on the floor. He stood there, curling his truck keys around his fingers.

All the food was out of the bags, scattered across every hard surface of the kitchen and Snow scanned the room calculating the ingredients she needed in her mind. Peas, carrots, onion, garlic, yams, bread, beef, thyme, marjoram—

But, wait a minute, where was the fruit? Hadn't she purchased peaches at the market?

No peaches meant no pie. No pie meant Snow had failed on her first task for Granny. And the girls would mock her, because she knew she'd feel the need to explain herself and she'd end up babbling all about it and probably blubbering. It was all her fault. Dinner was ruined. She felt herself growing dizzy, faint.

Stop it, Snow. Pull yourself together.

It was an absurd train of thought, she knew, but she couldn't disembark. It felt like the walls were closing in on her, like this was the last straw. And in that moment, over a forgotten fruit, Snow began sobbing into the skirt of her apron like a three year old child. It was humiliating.

She felt Hansel's strong arms around her. "Hey, don't cry. What's wrong?"

She shook her head.

"You never know, maybe I can fix it."

"No you can't."

"I can't if you don't tell me."

Hansel pulled Snow closer to his chest and stroked her

hair. His hand was warm, comforting. It felt like what had been missing in her life even before she came to Granny's.

Should she tell him that strange things had been happening to her? Things that made her question her very identity? Should she tell him that she felt trapped in this amusement park of a house and that she was afraid to go to sleep at night because a man with an ax kept showing up in her dreams? Should she tell him she was desperate for someone to talk to, that she was lonely, and that she longed for one true friend, one true love?

"Peaches," she croaked.

"Excuse me?"

Snow dried her tears with her apron and pulled away from Hansel. "I was going to make a peach pie. I forget the fruit."

Hansel's brow wrinkled. "Fruit. For a pie. That's the problem?" He said it as if he didn't believe her.

Snow nodded furiously, sticking to her story. "Yep. That's it."

Hansel smiled. "Well that's no problem at all. Come on, I've been wanting to show you this."

He grabbed her arm and yanked her through the back door. He practically ran all the way around to the other side of the house, dragging Snow along.

"What's all the fuss about?" she asked, breathless.

Hansel stopped and pointed. "There. Look. Isn't it gorgeous? They aren't even in season yet. It's like it grew overnight." Hansel looked at Snow. "Around the time you arrived, actually. Isn't it something?"

Snow felt every nerve in her body tingle. She inched closer, mesmerized by the beauty, the colors, the bounty. It was drawing her closer, step by step, and with every step, her heart beat faster until it was drumming in her chest. Then she was standing directly in front of it.

An apple tree. The largest, most beautiful fruit tree she had ever seen. Its leaves a more brilliant green than the grass beneath her feet. The fruit shiny, plump, and red as rubies. The trunk a rich cocoa color, and branches that reached out for yards like prickly fingers.

Hansel plucked a piece of the fruit from a low hanging branch and tossed it at Snow. She caught it.

And in that instant, everything changed.

SLEEPWALKING BEAUTY

A jolt of electricity surged through Snow White. It felt like every fiber of her being was hypersensitive to the sights, sounds, emotions, and sensations of the world around her. Her head was spinning as if this land was trying to shake her off.

Thoughts, images, and pictures, surged through her mind one after the other like a slide show, each more vivid than the last. Trees, a forest, a cottage, a glass coffin, the faces of forgotten friends—and old enemies. There was a crown—her crown, a castle she used to live in, a kingdom she once ruled. The man with the ax, the queen with an ax to grind, and the mirror that knew all of their deepest secrets.

She remembered.

Snow looked at Hansel. "Cut it down!" An order.

Hansel cocked his head. "Excuse me?"

Snow had to think fast. Here—wherever *here* was—she was no longer a leader, she was a criminal.

"I, I mean, I'm allergic." She backed away. "Maybe you could ask Granny if it can be removed."

She didn't wait for his answer. She just turned and ran back toward the house.

Punzie was still lounging by the pond. "Hey Princess, where's the fire?"

Snow realized she was still clutching the apple. She wound up a pitch and fired it at Punzie's head.

"Ow, dammit!" Punzie rubbed the back of her head where the apple smacked it. "I'm going to kick your ass for that." She stood up.

Easy, Snow. Tread lightly until you figure out what's happening.

She stopped. "Sorry, thought you'd like a snack. Just picked it. Didn't mean to hit you." Although she had.

Punzie glared at her, but she must have decided it wasn't worth the effort to chase Snow up the hill. She sat back down on the grass next to Bob. Snow watched the apple roll into the pond. There was a faint bubbling, a burst of water like a fountain, then it was gone.

Snow slapped through the screen door. She ran down the hallway and up the stairs, anger boiling through her veins with each step.

If her hunch was right—and as the appointed leader of the United Kingdoms of Enchantment, her hunches were usually right—then the woman in the room she was about to barge into had a lot of explaining to do. After all, she was the only one who had seemed to be even remotely in touch with her personal nemesis.

The look on her face, her reaction when Snow pulled that wheel from the closet—that couldn't have been a coincidence. She had to have felt *something*.

Snow tested the handle. It wasn't locked.

She opened the door and several images hit her all at once. Aura asleep on her bed, a bandage around one finger. A spinning wheel—not the one from Granny's forbidden closet, but another, sitting beneath the window. The window wide open, a blue jay perched on the sill.

"No!" Snow rushed over to Aura Rose and shook her shoulders. "Wake up! Aura, wake up!"

The princess didn't open her eyes. Snow dashed to the bathroom, grabbed a glass of water and ran back to Aura's room. She splashed it on her face, jumped on her chest, and slapped her. Hard.

She raised her other hand just as Aura grabbed it.

"If you hit me again, I'm going to throw you out of that fucking window."

Snow gasped. "You're awake! Thank God!"

"No, thank you, Snow. A bitch slap usually interrupts my sleep pretty effectively. What the hell are you *doing*?" Aura shoved Snow off of her and sat up. She looked at her shirt. "Why am I wet?"

"I thought, I thought...the spinning wheel...." Snow wasn't sure what to say. Had it happened to Aura too? The visions, the flashes. Did she remember who she was? Is that why she was so frightened of the spinning wheel yesterday?

Aura got off the bed. "That was a gift from one of the Meals on Wheels clients."

Snow looked at her.

"Old people." Aura shrugged. "Always trying to get rid of crap they don't need." She laughed. But her voice shook as if she was nervous.

Snow approached the wheel. She noticed the needle was taped over with paper towels.

She turned back to Aura. "You remember, don't you?"

Aura averted her eyes. She shuffled to the door, closed it, and stuck a chair beneath the knob.

She didn't turn around for a long while and Snow got the suspicion that she was trying to compose herself.

"I don't know what you mean by *remember*, but something

has been happening to me. Ever since I helped you clean out that stupid closet...I feel like I'm going crazy."

Snow said gently, "You're not going crazy."

Aura began pacing. "I keep seeing things, hearing things... voices that aren't there. And there's this horrible woman who haunts my dreams."

Snow said, "Does she carry a staff and wear a black cape? With thorns?"

Aura's eyes widened. She stopped and stared at Snow. "How did you know that?"

Snow could have tried to explain it, but it was clear to her that Aura wasn't quite on the same page. Snow was the first princess. It stood to reason that she would be the first to see through the veil of this world, no matter who created it. She decided it was best to show Aura Rose who she truly was.

Snow enveloped Aura's hands in hers. "Aura, how did the wheel get in your room?"

"Hansel carried it up for me. I was afraid someone would think I stole it, so I asked Hansel to bring it up to my room this morning." She looked at Snow nervously. "I don't even recall driving home. There was this...flash of light, a boom, and then I was here."

Snow couldn't make sense of that. Some sort of power surge perhaps? Surely the wheel must have magic, as the apples seem to. Energy can be affected by it. Then Snow realized something. "Wait...you carried it to your car last night? Did you touch the wheel?"

"Not the wheel itself. The woman who gave it to me had it wrapped up in a blanket."

So she hadn't touched the surface. Snow had touched the apple with both hands. Touching the apple was never going to hurt her, but eating it would surely have killed her. So maybe, as long as Aura steered clear of the needle and touched just the wheel, her memories would return, as Snow's had.

"I need you to touch the spinning wheel with both hands." Snow said.

Aura shook her head, her lips pursed. "Uh-uh. No way." She edged backwards.

Snow said, "Please, just trust me. Everything will be clear if you do."

Aura looked doubtful.

"I promise you, Aura, if you do this, you won't feel crazy anymore. You'll feel relieved, strong." And really, really confused, but why spoil the surprise?

Aura considered this.

Snow urged her on. "I'll be right here the whole time."

When Aura didn't move, Snow said, "You've stolen cars, you've beat up your parole officer, and you have the mouth of a miner. Are you really afraid of a piece of wood?"

That did it. Aura made a face at Snow as she trudged forward. She put her hands up, then down, then up again.

Snow had the urge to push her, but that wasn't her style. Aura glanced over her shoulder.

"You can do it," Snow said.

And she did.

THE BETTER TO AX YOU WITH

J udge Redhood had just settled down to watch her favorite picture show, *The Wolf That Stole Her Heart*, when she heard tires screeching outside. Fang lifted his head and growled. "Go back to sleep, Fang. I'm sure it's nothing to be alarmed about. Probably just Tink reporting in for work." Her assistant didn't always come home on her evenings off and the judge never asked where she had been. She assumed the girl enjoyed camping.

Fang grumbled, then rolled onto his back and closed his eyes.

The judge heard the door bang open with a clatter. She got off the couch reluctantly to scold her assistant and to ask her to make a bowl of ice cream.

When she arrived at the door, the judge saw Tink and Robin Hood standing in her foyer, each of them looking like something the wolf had dragged in.

"What in the world? Tink, what happened to you? Your —" She almost said her glitter was gone, but she stopped herself in time. "I mean, you look upset."

The fairy's shadow was detached too. It slumped to the side as if it had a broken...something.

"I am upset. I was having a lovely dinner at the café last night, but that stupid Aura ruined it."

The judge brightened at this. "She did?"

Robin Hood eyed the judge suspiciously, so she set her face to a frown.

Tink said, "She came in to speak with Doc Bean and she ruined his dinner and my time with him."

Judge Redhood crossed her arms. "Is that so?" She looked at Robin.

"Nothing illegal. And she was where she was supposed to be delivering a meal after that," Robin said.

Tink glared at Robin. "Nothing illegal? Well, then it should be a crime to curse and raise your voice to a pillar of the community." She tapped her tiny foot and cast her gaze on the judge. "And she poured beer on his perfectly good turkey."

Robin said, "Again, not a crime."

The judge paced. Perhaps instilling the laws of this land rather than creating her own had been a mistake. It had seemed the best option should a native somehow crash through the barrier. There was no magic here, they made sure of that. Except for the minimal amount she brought with her and that was closely guarded. It was why they chose this land to banish the princesses in the first place. If there was magic, then the spell that had been cast from her own realm could be broken from within. And magic in the hands of the princesses would be disastrous, even deadly, for all of them.

"Judge, did you hear me?" Tink asked.

"What?" Redhood said.

"I said I followed Aura. I think she was up to something." Tink's eyes grew even bigger. "Something sneaky."

Robin stepped forward. "Yeah, about that."

There was a mustard stain on his shirt and his hat was crooked. He was heavier than when the judge had been married to him, and he looked unhappy. Perhaps Marion wasn't the perfect woman after all. Served him right. How dare he leave her! Everything she'd done, she'd done for their marriage. And he walked away just because of a few disagreements? All couples fight, for Pete's sake. Perhaps not all wives shoot their husbands with a crossbow, but still. She wondered if he still had the scar. He didn't limp here like he did back home.

"I have a real problem with your assistant interfering with my job," Robin said.

The judge lifted her brow at Tink.

Tink made a pouty face and crossed her arms. "Well *he* doesn't seem to be too interested. He never finds them at fault for anything."

Robin shot a glare at Tink. "That's because technically, they haven't broken any laws. And frankly, young lady, you damn near did by interfering with my investigation."

Tink's face grew so red, the judge thought smoke might blow out her ears at any moment. "Why, that is cockadoodle lie!"

Robin rolled his eyes and said, "Judge, would you please have a word with her and make this stop? I gotta get home to the wife."

Something dark shifted inside the judge at the sound of Robin calling another woman his wife. She watched as the man who didn't remember sharing a bed with her once upon a time turned to walk out of her house.

She looked at Tink, full of fire and vinegar and gung-ho to find even the tiniest infraction that would send one of the princesses back to jail. And she made a decision.

Robin was too soft. Too fair. Always trying to do the right

thing no matter who it hurt. She hated that. "Mr. Hood," she said as he was about to leave.

Robin turned. "Yeah."

"You're fired."

A look of shock swept over Tink's pixie face. She made a mewing sound.

"Come again?" Robin said.

"Your services are no longer required," said the judge.

"Now wait just a damned minute." Robin's jaw hardened, his eyes blazed. "You can't fire me."

Damn, but he was still sexy when he was angry.

The judge cocked her head. "As an officer of the court, and the mayor of Everafter, I most certainly can."

Boy, was she glad she'd had the sense to implement her own hierarchy.

Robin looked at Tink. Tink shuffled her feet on the tile as if she wished it would open up and swallow her.

Robin slowly walked up to the judge and stood inches from her face. She could feel the heat of him. His anger leapt off his chest and penetrated her heart. It excited her in places where she hadn't felt anything in a long time.

In a low voice that made her insides squishy and her knees rattle, he said, "You know, I get the feeling this is personal for you. Why is that?"

She didn't respond. Didn't even blink. She couldn't. He had that kind of power over her when he was in this state of mind.

Robin smiled ruefully and lifted his hat. "Well then, I guess I'll never know."

It didn't sound like a retreat. It sounded like a threat.

Robin turned and tipped his hat to Tink. "Good luck, young lady. You're gonna need it."

The cowboy walked out of the house and into the afternoon light. A wind gushed through the entryway and circled around both Tink and the judge. The door slammed shut, sending a shiver through Judge Redhood's core.

She stood there wondering if she'd just made a huge mistake.

Tink said, "Do you want to hear my report?"

WELCOME TO FAR, FAR AWAY

S now watched as Aura slowly turned around. She studied her face, looking for some recognition. *Come on, Aura. I know you're in there.*

Neither of them spoke for several moments. Finally, Aura said, "What the hell happened, Snow? How did we get here?"

Snow beamed, relieved to have someone who was sharing this experience with her. They had never been friends *per se*, but after the wars they had come together, all five of them, seeking to end the fighting, the pillaging, the loss of their people. The treaty they had signed in their own blood was mutually agreed upon and beneficial to all the lands. Snow knew in her heart of hearts that her fellow royal sisters couldn't be behind this. The United Kingdoms of Enchantment meant everything to them. They had achieved what none of the royal families that came before them could. Peace.

"I don't know, but we need to figure it out and fast. We have to get back home," Snow said.

What damage had been done in their absence? And who

would want to destroy what they had worked so hard to build?

Aura nodded. "Agreed." She looked out the window, her brow furrowed in concentration. "So what do we do in the meantime?"

"I suggest we act as if everything is normal. I don't know if the others know who they are yet. Best to wait and see. Then we can work on a plan."

Aura brushed her hair back. "So now what?"

Snow looked at her. "I guess now we cook dinner."

"We?"

Snow narrowed her eyes. "Yes. Do you take issue with that?"

"I thought you said 'act normal'. I never cooked back home, why should I start now?"

"Aura," Snow grumbled.

Aura raised her hands in defeat. "Fine. But I don't do desserts."

Snow said, "Yes, well neither do I tonight."

The former princesses of the United Kingdoms of Enchantment compared notes for a little while before heading to the kitchen to cook dinner. They discussed who in the town they recognized from Enchantment. There was Robin Hood, of course—longtime defender of citizen's rights. Red Riding Hood, who somehow ended up a judge in this land, which, given her history, baffled Snow. Hansel, who had been betrothed to Cindy before her stepmother traded her hand in marriage. She wanted a place in high society and, unfortunately for Cindy, chose a Prince who turned out to favor men over women. Gretel, Hansel's sister, whom the princesses had appointed to lead the royal army after she caught and captured three wicked witches and uncovered a plot to kill Snow White.

Snow said, "Do you know who Granny is? I don't recognize her."

Aura shook her head. "I don't, but I tell you, something feels familiar about her."

Snow didn't share that vibration. "You'll need to work on discovering her identity then."

Aura nodded.

It was getting late, so they decided to get started on dinner. The most important dinner of their lives.

As they walked towards the door and Aura removed the chair lodged beneath the doorknob, she said, "Snow. Do you think it's possible...I mean..." Aura's eyes clouded. She whispered. "Do you think it's one of them behind this?"

She didn't have to ask *who*. She knew exactly who Aura meant. The thought drifted there in her mind, Aura's words floating freely. Snow White didn't even want to entertain the possibility that one of her blood sisters would betray her like this. And for what? To leave her kingdom, her home, her people for this drab world? For a life behind bars. A life where she answered to a higher court.

She didn't want to think that it could be true. But she also decided that it would be foolish to completely rule it out. She answered Aura honestly. "I don't know."

They cooked in silence, keeping an eye on the clock and watching the door for their housemates and Granny. The mood in the house had darkened. The air felt heavier to Snow as she bustled about the stove, adding vegetables to the pot, slicing butter for the bread, making iced tea.

The sun had melted beyond the horizon and she turned on a light switch. The florescent bulb reminded Snow of the timepiece closet. What did it mean, all those clocks and watches and numbers? And what of the mysterious ballroom that had drawn her to it? She recognized the mirror now, of course. The mirror that had appeared as if from thin air that showed her who she once was, for it belonged to her now. It hung in her palace back in Enchantment as a stark reminder that evil walked among them. That no matter who she *thought* she could trust, a princess was never safe. Especially one who held power.

Which meant, none of them were safe. Not even here at Granny's house.

So *who* was Granny? What did she have to do with any of this? And what was she hiding behind the locked door for which there was no key to open?

Snow glanced over at Aura. She was setting the table, placing the napkins and cutlery, glassware and dinner plates in front of each chair. If Aura had felt a spark of familiarity with Granny, then the old woman had to be someone from the sleeping princess's past. She wanted to ask, but she didn't dare for fear that someone would walk in unexpectedly.

As she fried the garlic and onion, Snow spotted Cotton dash by, a piece of cheese in his mouth, off to have a feast of his own. He ran down the hallway that led to the first forbidden room Bella had pulled Snow into to talk.

Bella. What did she know? Had she felt something in the ballroom? Or had that been Snow's imagination? She was comforted to see there was at least some form of Beast here. Even if the dog wasn't really Bella's "Beast". He had always protected Bella in their land. And he always would. Loyal to the end—that was Beast.

But what exactly did the bookish princess mean by that "partners in crime" crack?

Snow blew out a sigh and Aura glanced at her, flashing a shaky smile. Snow supposed she trusted her, for now at least, but what if it wasn't a coincidence that Aura regained her memory around the time Snow had? What if that was the plan?

What if there was no one she could trust?

Cindy seemed to have a true disdain for Snow, although Hansel assured her that it was the divorce that had changed the slippered princess. Snow found that amusing. Cindy had been forbidden to divorce Prince Trevor back home when his father, the king, was still alive. It wasn't until years after she came into power, after the treaty was signed, that the laws were changed. In fact, she had been about to file the paperwork to be rid of her prince forever before...

Before what? What brought them to this?

She thought back to the scene the mirror had shown her of the soldiers dragging her away. Did she recognize them? Were they soldiers of Enchantment? Her personal men? Members of Gretel's army? She couldn't place their faces or their uniforms, but perhaps her memory was fuzzy from whatever had transpired to bring her here. She certainly didn't recall ever being dragged off in shackles.

Or was that a vision of a future event? The kitchen was getting hotter the longer she cooked, so Snow walked over to the back door to let some air flow through the room. She could see the pond from where she stood and she thought of Punzie and Bob the frog. Strange how the frog would follow her around. Punzie's plague was the tower, her strength her hair. There was no frog in her story. So why would a frog follow her in this land?

Snow was arranging the bread in a basket as she thought about what would happen in group therapy tomorrow. She would have to reveal her crimes and they theirs, so did that mean things would change when they returned home?

If they returned home.

The thought of sitting in a circle and revealing to her fellow stateswomen her crimes and—

Snow dropped the basket. "Oh my God."

Aura looked up. "What?"

She looked at Aura. "Jack."

The meaning of that one name slapped them both in the face.

IF THE SHOE FITS

B east and Bella wandered into the kitchen, and Bella stuck her head in the refrigerator to find some dinner for the dog. She settled on leftover meatloaf and gravy, cracked an egg on top, mixed it all up, and fed Beast outside.

When she came back into the kitchen, the empty bowl in her hand, she wore a confused look. "Did you guys see that apple tree? The thing is huge now. How the hell did that happen?"

Snow and Aura exchanged a nervous glance. Snow said, "Fertilizer. Hansel's a master gardener I guess."

Bella stole a glance back at the screen door. She turned to Snow, skepticism crawling all over her face. "Really? Is he also a wizard? Because trees don't grow overnight."

Snow shrugged. "How should I know? I only arrived a few days ago."

Aura grabbed a bottle of wine from the table and poured herself a healthy glass. Bella's eyes followed her.

"Aura?"

Aura drank half the glass in a few gulps. "What?"

"The tree. Out back. Did you see it?"

She shifted her eyes to the table, feigning interest in the flowers Snow had put in a vase. "I avoid nature at all costs, Bella, you know that. Since when are you so interested in the landscaping?" She finished her wine and poured herself another glass.

Bella crossed her arms defensively. Aura was appealing to Bella's lackadaisical attitude about the house and Snow hoped it would work. They certainly couldn't explain things to her yet, not until they had a better handle on them.

Bella narrowed her eyes, clearly not used to being challenged. "Well, I'm not, but when a tree as tall as a skyscraper appears from nowhere, I notice. It's called being observant. And why are you acting like a bitch on wheels?"

Punzie and Bob came into the kitchen then. Punzie said, "She's still pissed that I put a frog in her bed, aren't you, Sticky Fingers?"

Aura whirled on Punzie. "That was you?" Then she spotted Bob and jumped onto a chair. "What's it doing back in the house?" She was doing the creepy-crawly dancing thing again.

Punzie said, "He lives here now. We've bonded. Get used to it."

"Snow..." Aura whined.

Punzie and Bella looked at each other. Punzie said, "Oh, like Miss Priss here is going to rescue you. Right."

Snow gave Aura a slight shake of her head. To the others she said, "I helped Aura out by taking, er, Bob outside earlier. No big deal."

Punzie pulled a chair out and poured herself a glass of wine. "Well he's my friend and I say he stays."

Snow said, "That's fine. Perhaps not around the dinner table, though."

Bella's look of amusement told Snow that she was calculating how many seconds would pass before Punzie cold-cocked her.

Punzie gathered her braid in front of her, swinging it like a jump rope. "Who died and made you queen bitch?"

Uh-oh.

Back in Enchantment, the other four princesses had appointed Snow the peace ambassador of the kingdoms for precisely these types of situations. Snow had a knack for dispelling disputes and interjecting reason into any argument, and the rest of the princesses knew that if they were to get anything done they would need someone to act as a mediator.

But they weren't in Enchantment anymore. Here, they thought Snow was meek as a mouse. Much as she hated it for now, she would have to play that role.

Snow raised her arms. "Do what you want, but when Granny comes home, I don't think she'll be too happy to find a frog in her kitchen."

Punzie frowned. She looked down at Bob. He gazed up at her with adoration. "Damn, you're right. I wore my leopard platforms one time to Sunday dinner and she confiscated them right there. I still haven't found where she hid them."

Snow, hoping to gain another recruit in her off-limits rooms expedition said, "I might be able to help with that." She shot Aura a conspiratorial look.

Bella said, "Mission spic and span is still on the agenda, I take it."

Punzie flipped her braid over her neck. "What are you talking about?"

Bella thumbed at Snow. "Princess Curious over here has her panties in a bunch over the condition of this giant fire hazard and she thinks there's some deep dark secret in the 'Do Not Enter' rooms."

Punzie rolled her eyes. "You mean Granny's rooms o'

crap." She looked at Snow. "Have you seen the garbage she hauls in from those flea markets? Some of that shit literally had fleas in it."

Snow gave Bella a questioning glance.

Bella said, "It's true. I had to hose down Beast with five gallons of flea dip a couple of weeks ago." She reached for a slice of bread. "And that is not a fun task, believe me." She plopped herself in a chair and buttered her bread. "It's like washing an elephant with an ornery disposition."

Punzie said, "Well, I certainly don't want Bob to end up in a closet, so I guess I'll take him to my room before Granny gets home."

Cindy ushered into the kitchen, breathless. She was wearing dark sunglasses, a trench coat, and stiletto heels.

"Speaking of closets," Punzie said as she brushed past Cindy and into the hallway.

"Piss up a rope, pole girl," Cindy snapped over her shoulder. She rushed over to the table. "So she's not home yet? I'm not late?"

Snow said, "No, you're right on time."

"Whew, thank the god of shoes." Cindy poured herself a glass of wine.

Bella smirked at her, crossing her arms. "You think that's wise?"

"Not now, Bella. I need this to calm my nerves." She downed the whole glass and slammed it on the table. She pulled her sunglasses down and looked around the room.

Aura stepped down from the chair. "What's wrong with you? You look like a flasher."

Cindy pointed at her. "You would be especially proud."

"I doubt that, but I'm intrigued. Go on."

Cindy swung her head around the room again. She went to the back door, closed and locked it. Then she skittered back to the table. She untied her coat and said, "Look what I've got."

Bella gave Cindy a sarcastic smile. "We all saw what you've got the last time we went to Witch's Brew. The entire bar saw what you've got."

"Funny." Cindy smirked.

Bella shrugged. "I try."

Cindy pulled out a black leather box about the size of a shoe box. There was a pink silk ribbon wrapped around it with a crisp tag dangling from it. Judging from the number on the tag and the tiny picture of a shoe, it seemed that a shoe box was exactly what it was, although Snow had never seen such elaborate packaging for a pair of pumps.

"Check it out. Doesn't it look delicious?"

They gathered around the table to examine Cindy's new treasure.

"Shoes." Aura shrugged. "Why would that impress me?"

Cindy gave Aura an exasperated look as Snow stepped forward for a better view.

"Not just any shoes." She glanced from one woman to the other. "I stole them from the shop." She bit her bottom lip and giggled.

"You lifted a pair of shoes from your ex-husband's store? He's a gazillionaire, Cindy." Bella rolled her eyes at Cindy's frown. "But hey, Trevor 26 million, Cindy one." She gave her two thumbs up. "Good job."

Cindy put her fist on her hip. "Honey, you may know books, but you don't know shit about shoes." She turned the box around and lifted it up to reveal a photograph of what looked like a pair of four inch heels made entirely from diamonds.

Snow gasped and swung her head to Aura. They exchanged a wide-eyed look. They knew those shoes. They were the foundation of Cindy's story.

"One of a kind Hilda Cobbler crystalline pumps with an unbreakable diamond heel and a sapphire bow. She only made one pair in a few sizes." Cindy clapped her hands.

Snow clutched her stomach.

Another nemesis. First, it was the poisoned apple from Snow's story. Then it was the spinning wheel from *Sleeping Beauty*. And now, Cinderella's glass slipper.

How were these items finding their way to the princesses? To Everafter? The original cursed artifacts had been locked in a vault back in Enchantment, sealed, along with their written biographies. There was talk of destroying them, but the princesses had been warned that the consequences of doing so were unknown. It could be devastating not only to the women themselves, but to their kingdoms, to history, and anyone else their stories touched. The risk was too great.

Were those pieces still locked away in Enchantment? Or had they been stolen? Could a seed from the original apple have been planted here in Granny's yard? Could the spinning wheel have broken through whatever veil cloaked Everafter? Was someone sending them the links to their lives?

And if so, to what end?

Cindy said, "I didn't even try them on yet, I just grabbed them and bolted." She ran her slender fingers along the box, practically purring. "You want to see them?"

Snow and Aura shouted at the same time. "No!"

GUESS WHO'S NOT COMING TO DINNER?

G ranny was late.

Throughout the course of the evening, the other women mentioned a few times how rare it was for Granny to be late for Sunday dinner and that she had never, ever missed the meal entirely. Snow wondered for the umpteenth time who Granny was exactly. And what was keeping her.

"Where do you suppose she is?" Snow asked around nine p.m. to no one in particular.

Cindy was on her second bottle of wine. "Who knows? Maybe she broke down and hit the Bingo tables."

Punzie said, "Nah, I don't think so. Granny slayed that dragon a long time ago."

"Well if you don't feed me soon, someone will need to carry me upstairs." Cindy hiccupped.

Aura shot a look at Snow and she knew precisely what it meant. *Fine with me.* Earlier, while rummaging for the corkscrew she had tossed in a drawer, Snow and Aura had hatched a plan to confiscate Cindy's shoes and hide them. They didn't think she was ready for the truth yet, least of all in her inebriated state. If she needed help getting to bed, it would be the perfect opportunity to take them, as Cindy had stashed the slippers away in her room hours ago.

Snow got up from the table and said, "All right, dinner won't stay fresh much longer anyway." She looked at Aura, pointedly.

Aura poured more wine into Cindy's glass.

Bella said, "I'll help."

Snow didn't think much of it until Bella pinned her in front of the stove. "Okay, something stinks around here and I don't mean your perfume."

Snow snapped her head toward Bella. She wasn't certain if she was more surprised that Bella seemed to be accusing her of something or that she didn't like Snow's scent. It was herbal. Reminiscent of the smell of cut grass. Everyone liked the smell of cut grass. It was a fact.

"I don't know what you're talking about," Snow said.

"There is something going on with you and Aura, and I want to know what it is right now." Bella's eyes blazed.

Snow squirmed away from her. She didn't want to get into any of this with Bella any more than she did Cindy, or Punzie for that matter. In due time, she would try to sort out this mess, but right now she didn't have all the answers. Heck, she hardly had *any* answers. What was she supposed to tell her? *You're actually a royal princess, leader of an enchanted kingdom that has magic and beauty far beyond your wildest dreams, but somehow we've all been sucked into this dreary other-world where we're treated as common criminals. Oh and your dog? There's a good chance he may have once been your prince.*

Snow said, "I helped her get rid of a frog. She helped me clean out a closet. You know this already."

Bella leaned in a bit closer and lowered her tone. "I think you're full of shit. I think there's something more going on, and I want to know what it is."

Bella had always been a force to reckon with, but deep down Snow knew that although she was fierce, she was also fair. She wasn't the violent type, but if there was one thing that drove Bella mad, it was being out of the loop. Being denied access to records, information, news, stories. She must have been having some sort of a breakdown without books—her outlet for her obsessive compulsive yearning for knowledge.

Snow said, "Okay fine, I offered to, um..."

Think, Snow.

"To what?"

Snow had no idea. She hadn't thought the lie through. She bit her lip. "Uh..."

Aura walked up and whispered, "You're not telling her our little secret, are you, Snow?"

Snow felt her eyes grow to saucer size as she looked at Aura. "Certainly not."

What was Aura up to?

Aura cocked her head back toward the table where Punzie and Cindy sat.

"Snow's going to help me get back at Punzie."

Bella leaned closer and smiled. "Really, how?"

Aura nudged Snow. "Tell her."

"Right, um..." Peanut dashed by just as Snow glanced down at the floor. His whiskers twitched as he stopped to squeak at her. "Mice! Lots of mice. In her bed."

Bella made a face. "Ew. Count me out."

Punzie called, "Hey, can we eat sometime before Flasher Barbie over here climbs up on the table?"

"Afraid I'll give you a run for your money, Punzie?" Cindy spilled some wine as she stood up and jutted her hips to a tune that must have been playing in her own head.

"Oh, please. Like you could *balance* on a stage, let alone dance on one." Punzie snorted.

Cindy wagged her finger at Punzie. "I'm going to ignore that partially because I'm feeling great about screwing over Trevor and partially because at the moment, that might be true."

Snow clapped her hands. "Okay, no sense waiting for Granny any longer."

She reached into the refrigerator and pulled out the salad and dressing. Bella grabbed the vegetables and pot roast, and Aura rummaged around in a drawer for serving utensils.

They ate in relative silence, with nothing but the tick of the clock and the scrape of cutlery on plates interrupting the calm.

It was clear they were all wondering the same thing.

Where was Granny?

THE NEXT MORNING, Snow was awakened by a soft rapping. She threw the covers off and climbed out of bed, shuffling to the door. Aura whispered, "Snow, it's me."

She opened the door to discover a frantic-looking Aura standing before her. Dark rings drew circles around her green eyes, her hair was tied into a frenzied knot, and she was wearing the same clothes she'd had on the night before.

She rushed into the room and closed the door behind her softly.

Snow yawned and rubbed the sleep from her eyes. "You look as if you haven't slept a wink."

"I haven't." Aura scurried to the window to cover it with a pillowcase and spun back toward Snow. She grabbed a small bottle from her back pocket, unscrewed the cap and gulped its contents. It had the word 'energy' slashed across it in pointy blue letters.

Aura wiped her mouth and Snow said, "Aura, why don't you have a seat? You look like you could use a rest."

Aura cracked her neck and danced in place. She jabbed the air a few times. "I'm fine—just need to stay awake long enough to get through group."

Right, it was Monday. The first day they would all attend therapy together.

Snow felt a concrete weight settle into her stomach. She was dreading the session. Dreading seeing Jack again. Especially knowing that he had no idea who she was.

Or did he?

One problem at a time, Snow.

"What kept you up all night, Aura?"

Aura jittered around the room like a buzzing fly. She opened Snow's closet and filtered through the few belongings hanging from the rod.

"I was waiting up for Granny. I wanted to see if somehow I could recognize her, lift a vibe from her or a memory, anything that would fill a piece of this fucked-up puzzle."

Snow watched as Aura shut the closet, wondering what the heck the princess was doing, but understanding that the woman was already on the edge.

"And?"

Aura opened the desk drawer. "And what?" She lifted up Cotton's blanket as he slept. He made a soft mewing sound and rolled over.

Snow tapped her foot. "Did you uncover her identity?"

Aura was on the floor now, her head lodged under the desk. "No. And do you know why?"

"Enlighten me."

Aura stuck her head out. "Because she never came home."

Snow's mouth dropped. "What?"

Aura crawled out from beneath the desk and went to inspect under the bed. "Yep." Her voice was muffled as she shimmied her narrow hips under the squeaky metal frame. "First time since I've been here that she hasn't come home at all."

A sinking sensation swept over Snow. This was bad. Very bad. She felt it instinctively. Once upon a time, Snow White hadn't followed her instincts, and because she was more trusting of others than her own self, it got her...well, killed, actually. After that experience, she'd vowed never to ignore her gut feelings again.

Granny was involved in their predicament one way or another.

So was she a friend? Or a foe?

Aura was now rifling through Snow's empty suitcases.

Snow said, "Do you mind telling me what you're doing?"

Aura frowned and dropped the tweed suitcase. She planted her hands on her hips and looked around the room. "Checking for bugs."

Snow stiffened, "I'll have you know this space is cleaner than an operating room."

Aura rolled her eyes, "Lighten up, Your Highness. I was talking about the electronic kind." She tapped her ear. "Listening devices."

They were standing in the smallest, tidiest room in the house. If there had been any such article present, Snow would have found it, and she said as much to Aura.

"I figured. I swept the house last night and came up with nothing. It's clean. And I found nothing in Granny's room to tell us who she really is or anything to indicate she was plotting against us. Just a whole lot of receipts from flea markets and a book inventorying all of her junk."

"Do you have it?" Snow asked.

Aura reached into her back pocket and tossed a spiral bound notebook to Snow. She flipped through a few pages then looked at Aura. "So what do you suppose any of this means?"

Aura bent over and shook her arms and shoulders, raking her fingers through her long hair. When she stood up, she faced Snow with a solemn expression. "It means Granny's one of the good guys. And I think—"

The realization of what Aura was proposing charged at Snow. "One of the bad guys took her."

Aura's eyes glistened and her lips fell into a grim line as she nodded.

Snow stood and tucked the notebook into her desk for the time being. "We have to find her."

AN APPLE A DAY WON'T KEEP
ROBIN AWAY

R obin Hood was a creature of habit, and as a creature of habit he adhered to a certain routine. For instance, every Monday morning he wrote a list of all the workout routines he planned to do that week, followed by a strict diet, void of sugar and carbohydrates. And every Monday he kissed his wife, skipped the gym, picked up a chocolate éclair, and headed out to visit the girls of Granny's House to ensure that they attended their anger management session. It wasn't a perfect system, but it worked for him.

You see, once Robin was assigned a job, be it lawman, parole officer, or dog catcher, he was compelled to follow that job through to the end no matter what. He couldn't help himself. So a little thing like getting fired by the biggest bitch in Everafter wasn't going to stop him from doing his job. He may no longer have a badge, or a legally issued firearm, or even an identification card with his job title written on it in bold block letters, but he had his dignity. Mostly.

So when he spotted Tink's car, which was the size of a go-cart, wedged between a lilac bush and a dog house near

Granny's home, Robin was so angry he considered crashing into her.

He didn't. Instead, he coasted on by as if he was just passing through the neighborhood. His assessment was that she wasn't up to a whole lot because she was fast asleep in the back seat. Her face was scrunched up against the window like a suction-cupped stuffed animal, her turquoise hair floated over her shoulders, and her thin arms were wrapped around her short legs.

She looked a little like a holiday ornament.

Robin parked his own car across the street behind a large truck and reached for his binoculars.

The house was quiet, which wasn't unusual for this hour. The women still had some time before they had to be at Dr. Bean's office for group. A light flickered on in the bathroom for a brief moment, then went out. He shifted his gaze to the driveway. All the cars were accounted for except Granny's.

Odd. Granny wasn't what one might describe as an early bird, but perhaps she had gotten wind of a barn sale or something. Robin had never known a woman to collect so much junk in all his life. Where she put it he didn't know, because although he visited the house frequently, he never saw any new items. He didn't trail Granny often, as the judge had never asked him to, but he liked to be thorough, and since she was in charge of his parolees, he thought it best to at least gain some insight into the old woman and her habits.

He'd discovered only three things about Granny in the short time he'd known her. The first was that she talked as if she was reading a phrase book backwards. Like she had her own language that only she understood, and her audience had to decipher her meaning from context. He often wondered if the girls she took in were given some sort of decoder ring on move-in day. The second thing Robin knew about the woman was that she seemed to be as old as time itself. Lastly, Granny loved to shop, especially if it meant a good bargain, and especially if the junk she found was as old and worn as herself.

Granny seemed harmless enough. Just a sweet old lady trying to scrape by in life.

Robin unwrapped his éclair and took a hearty bite. The creamy vanilla filling squirted his shirt and he mopped it up with a napkin.

Something caught the corner of his eye as he tossed the napkins into the back seat. Two figures exited the back door of the looming house.

Robin twisted in his seat to get a better look of the back yard. It looked like Aura and the new girl, Snow, were taking a stroll. Both wore hoodies, long pants, and gloves. Odd for August, he thought. So not a stroll then. Were they going to do some gardening?

Robin adjusted the binoculars for a closer look and watched as the girls rounded the corner of the house.

That's when he saw it. An apple tree taller and wider than the dilapidated mansion, sprawled across the back yard. Robin studied the tree carefully, then lowered his binoculars. He couldn't recall ever seeing that tree before. Of course he didn't often stake out the back of the property, but Tink had taken his usual spot.

Robin put the binoculars back to his eyes, watching Snow and Aura approach the tree. Granny's women weren't exactly outdoorsy types, so he couldn't imagine what they were doing. They weren't very domesticated either, from what he had observed, although, now that he considered it, he didn't know the new girl all that well. Perhaps she wanted to bake a pie. Perhaps Aura was helping her.

Robin watched as Aura went to the back shed while Snow waited a few feet from the tree. She shuffled her feet impatiently, bit a fingernail off and chewed her lower lip, as if she were nervous just being around Aura.

"Looks, like you got the royal treatment, Snow White," he muttered. "So what was it? Snakes in your bed? A shove down the stairs? Or just a good old fashioned sucker punch?"

Robin took another bite of the pastry and washed it down with milk.

Aura returned with a chainsaw in her hand, and the two women had a discussion. Robin wished he could read lips, but that was a talent he'd never mastered. He could, however, read faces. Snow White looked to be completely in charge as she pointed to the tree and shoved a sack into Aura's free hand, then grabbed the chainsaw.

Aura shook her head, white knuckling the sack, but Snow wouldn't take no for an answer. She stepped forward, blocking Robin's view of Aura's face. Snow was pointing, her head bobbing up and down as if she were ordering Aura to do something.

Well this should be interesting. Robin had never known Aura to take orders from anyone. He wished he had some popcorn. If he were a betting man, he would have put twenty down on Aura to take Snow out in the third round with an uppercut.

To Robin's surprise, not only did Aura keep her hands to herself and her feet on the ground, but she stepped forward and looked up at the tree. She gave Snow a nervous glance back and Snow gave her a nod and a thumbs-up.

This was a plot twist Robin never saw coming. Aura taking orders? What was going on?

Aura reached her arm tentatively toward the tree and picked an apple. She buried it in the sack, shuddered, and reached for another. By the time she tied the sack up tight a few moments later, Robin had counted five apples.

Snow White stepped forward and patted Aura on the

back. She picked up the sack and set it a few feet away. Then she fired up the chain saw, grinning. She reached into her pocket and grabbed a pair of goggles and Aura did the same.

Snow tackled the tree like a pregnant woman tackles a carton of Rocky Road ice cream. There was no precision to her cuts, no rhyme or reason. She just hacked at it from every angle as if it had personally betrayed her until, after twenty minutes, the fruit tree crashed to the ground. The women high-fived each other.

Robin set his binoculars down and pulled out his notebook to record what he had just witnessed. When he looked up again, Snow and Aura were racing to the shed, Snow holding the chain saw, Aura carrying the sack.

Robin scratched his chin. "What are you bitches up to?"

Before he could even consider an answer, someone threw a rock at his windshield.

BETWEEN A ROCK AND A HARD FAE

W hen Snow emerged from the shed, she heard the distinct crack of glass and swung her head to see a girl with hair the color of a lagoon standing on the passenger side of Robin Hood's car, her tiny fists balled at her sides, her nostrils flaring.

"Who is that?" she asked Aura.

Aura followed Snow's gaze and said, "Oh. That's Tink of the Bluebells."

Snow looked at her. "The pixie? She's here too?"

"Yep." Aura closed and locked the shed, the sack of apples safely inside. "She works for the judge, or rather, Red Riding Hood." She looked at Snow, one eyebrow lifted. "And she has a huge crush on Jack."

Snow raised her own eyebrows. She stared at the young fairy as she wagged her tiny finger at Robin Hood through the window of his car. Robin got out of the Pinto and assessed the crack in his windshield. He ran his fingers through his hair and glared at Tink. Tink put her fists up, dancing all around him like a hungry mosquito. When she got close enough to take a swing, Robin straightened out his long arm and planted his hand on Tink's forehead. She continued to flail both arms at his stomach, missing each time.

"Do you suppose she has magic?" Snow asked.

Aura shrugged as the two climbed the small hill up and around the pond. "I don't think so. Look closely. Her wings are missing."

Snow frowned as Tink delivered a hard kick to Robin's shin. The lawman cried out and doubled over, rubbing the sore spot. This provided the fairy with an opportunity to pounce on his back. She dug her hands into his hair and bucked like she was wrestling a bull.

Snow supposed Aura was right, that Tink had been stripped of her glamour. But perhaps the apples would help them find magic. After all, they had to have sprung from some sort of spell, so there must be a thread that led from the fruit to a power source.

Because without magic, how in the world would they return home?

They approached the back door. Robin seemed to be losing his battle with the pixie. "Do you think we should help him?" Snow said. "After all, he is one of ours."

Aura thought about it. "Maybe, but I kind of want to see how this plays out."

Just as it seemed Robin might break free of his tiny tormentor, Tink stuck a thumb in his left eye. He howled.

"Why is he here, anyway?" Snow asked, still watching Robin's feeble attempts to defend himself.

Aura said, "Babysitting. He's here to make sure we attend our therapy."

"And Tink?" Snow asked just as she bit Robin's ear.

"That I'm not sure about."

Robin now appeared to be blinded in one eye, and his right ear was bleeding. The fairy seemed to revel in his pain.

She performed some sort of chop with her arm and let out a battle cry. Robin clutched his shoulder.

Snow said. "Enough is enough. This is undignified for a man of his caliber. We have to stop her."

Aura grabbed her arm and said in a low voice. "Okay, but just remember who he thinks we are." She pointed from Snow to herself. "Stay in the character that the puppet master, whoever it is, has created for us."

Snow nodded and set off to free the lawman of Enchantment.

As Robin Hood tried to fend off the fiend attacking him, he couldn't help but wonder what evil pact he might have made in a former life to bring him such humiliation. It was bad enough that the women of Granny's house got the better of him now and then. But at least they were strong, fierce women. To be beaten up by a girl the size of a garden gnome was just embarrassing. It didn't get any worse than that. At least, that's what he thought until he heard Aura's sarcastic tongue.

"You need a fly swatter there, Cowboy?"

Tink stopped wrestling for a moment. "This isn't your concern, Aura," she snapped in her squeaky-toy voice.

Aura walked closer and reached her hand up. She must have been putting the hurt on Tink in some capacity, because

Robin heard a squeal of pain. "I beg to differ, little one," she said. "You see, the cowboy and I have an understanding." Aura bent to look into Robin's good eye. "He pretends like I don't kick his ass on a regular basis, and I pretend he's not violating my civil rights by spying on me 24/7. Isn't that right, Mr. Parole Officer?"

Robin tried to roll his eyes, but it only caused him pain. He winced, and that hurt too.

Aura peeled Tink off Robin's back.

The tiny woman glared at Aura. "Well that's where you're wrong. He doesn't work for the city anymore."

Aura set the pixie down and glanced at Snow who kept her face stone still. "Is that so?" she asked.

Robin stood up, straightening his shirt. A trickle of blood ran down the front. How was he going to explain this to Marion?

Robin wished he had worn his hat. He felt more authoritative with his hat. "A misunderstanding," he said.

Tink's face was red as she said, "Not true! You were fired. I was there."

Aura crossed her arms. "Really?"

Robin felt a throbbing in his eye where Tink had tried to gouge it out, and his ear stung where she had bitten him. He tried to look assertive, but he was pretty sure he just looked like the victim of a car crash.

Tink said, "Yepper. I'm taking over now. The judge said." She stuck her chin out and crossed her tiny arms.

Aura laughed. "Okay, Tinker Toy." She looked at Snow. "This should be interesting."

Snow's mouth was set into a somber line. She was looking at Robin with an intensity he hadn't detected from the raven-haired woman during their first encounter. She looked almost....regal.

It intrigued him.

Aura glanced from Robin to Snow, then nudged her.

Snow lurched, recovered, and said in a demure voice, "Why don't you come inside. I can patch you up."

Robin met her eyes, softer now. Her lips relaxed into a welcome smile. As if there were two personalities behind her face.

He looked at Aura. She gave him a sly smile. "Princess here is more of a lover than a fighter." She winked.

Robin cleared his throat. "I appreciate that, Miss White, but I think I'll just be running along now. See to it you all make it to therapy." He looked at Tink, pointed. "I'll be having a word with your boss, Missy."

Tink scoffed at him.

For good measure, Robin added, "And Doctor Bean."

As Tink's face drained of all color and her grin fell, Robin couldn't help but feel a little smug that he had gotten in the last jab.

He got back into his car, started it up, and backed away from the women who seemed hell bent on torturing him.

As he drove down the street, he ventured a look back. The beautiful face of Snow White stared at him through the rearview mirror—her posture poised, her demeanor unshakable. She had the look of a woman who had lost something and was determined to get it back.

Robin had seen that look before. That resolve. He couldn't recall when or where, but he knew one thing.

It made him uneasy.

EVERYONE HAS A DEMON

J ack Bean was not a nervous man. On the contrary, he prided himself on being completely composed at all times. But as he twisted and re-knotted his tie, he felt a bit of that confidence slipping, and he wasn't certain why until he looked at his notes. Today was the day he would be treating Miss White for the first time.

The woman had an eerie effect on him when last he saw her and it seemed that now, as he was preparing for the group session, she had grabbed hold of him once again.

Why was that?

He had never, in all his professional career, been so intrigued by a patient.

What *was* it about her?

It couldn't just be that she was beautiful. All the women in Granny's house were striking. No, it was more than that. He had felt a connection to her. This, of course, was absurd because Jack wasn't connected to anyone and he liked his life that way. He found that people, and especially relationships, were messy and complicated. They caused pain, and Jack was not a fan of pain.

This was why Jack had devoted his life to helping others. As long as one kept a human connection, through work, volunteering, or some creative endeavor, one still contributed to the betterment of society—still hung on to the thread that is humanity. And surely that was a greater contribution than love.

Not that Jack had ever known love. At least none that was lasting.

In Jack's experience, both personally and professionally, abandonment was something the soul found difficult to overcome. Addiction, guilt, betrayal, even abuse—these are hallmarks of the human condition that can be built upon and repaired. But abandonment was hard to resolve, because it cannot be accessed from the psyche. It doesn't come from within the mind, but from deep inside the heart. People are conditioned from a young age to seek outside connections, approval, validation. *Belonging.* And when that is ripped away, it leaves a gaping hole in the very core of a person. One that Jack has helped others fill through his tireless work with some success. Although, if he were to be honest, he had not the patience to fill his own.

Which was one more reason he should keep a safe distance from Snow White.

He gave up on his tie altogether, and reminded himself that above all he was there for his patients, not himself.

The chirp of the women entering the therapy room infiltrated his office. He grabbed his notebook, opened the door, and stepped out to greet his patients.

BEFORE THE OTHERS joined them to walk to group therapy, Snow and Aura had discussed what they were going to do about Granny, Cindy's shoes, and Bella's nemesis—a sinister anthology that when read all the way to the end, sucked the reader into the twisted tales. The stories between the pages were the stuff of nightmares and it was through the loyalty and fierceness of Beast that she had survived her story at all. In fact, Bella had encountered Beast within the very pages of that storybook. He had been trapped there too, by an evil stepbrother who wanted to steal Beast's castle. Beast (whose given name was Bo) took cover in the shape of a terrifying creature the size of a small pony, with paws like a mountain lion's and a head like a gargoyle. Snow had no idea if the dog living in Granny's house was indeed Bella's Beast. She hoped not for his sake, but she suspected if he was, they would need a great deal of magic to expel him from his canine prison.

Since Bella's community service was reading to the elderly, Snow wondered if perhaps she already had encountered the book. Was it in Bella's possession? But if that were true, surely she would have read it, or at least touched it, for Bella couldn't resist the written word. And if she had read it through to the end, she wouldn't be here.

Aura pointed out that Bella didn't seem any different and Snow agreed that was true. Even if Snow's theory—that a simple two hand touch of the object of her story would jolt

Bella's memory as the apple had done with Snow's—Bella would have most likely confided in them. Or at least Snow.

Wouldn't she?

As they strolled along the sidewalk, Bob hopping alongside Punzie, Snow also thought about the long-haired princess's story nemesis. That would be harder to find. In her story, Punzie had been sentenced to solitary confinement by an evil queen who wanted her daughter to marry Prince Ashford. But Ashford loved Punzie. Had ever since they were children. Eventually he found her, and together they escaped the tower.

The queen was never heard from again.

Now, as the five princesses walked the streets of Everafter to meet with Jack, Snow paid special attention to the buildings along the route. Some of the Victorian homes dotting the landscape were designed with turrets, but nothing like the tower where Punzie had been imprisoned. There was an art gallery, featuring a painting of a leaning tower called Pisa, but that didn't come close to the monstrous place of Punzie's story. As they climbed the stairs of the community center, Snow wondered if perhaps Punzie's place of business hosted her story demon. She had never been there, of course. Maybe that's where they would find it.

Snow felt, deep inside her heart, that all of them needed to find their story horrors if they were ever to gain back their rightful thrones.

And that's when it hit Snow.

"The writer!" she said. Of course! He knew their biographies inside and out, top to bottom, word for word. Better than even the princesses themselves knew them. And he had, in fact, been the one to draw up the treaty for the United Kingdoms of Enchantment. Perhaps, if they could locate him, he might be able to lead them to Punzie's tower. Maybe even Bella's book. Or at least offer clues as to how to locate the objects of their stories.

That is, of course, if he was here, in Everafter. "And if he's still an ally."

Snow didn't realized she'd spoken aloud until Jack closed the door behind them.

"No. Just a doctor, I'm afraid," he said.

He smiled at her, his spectacles slightly slanted because one of his ears was a smidge higher than the other. His grin a bit lopsided, because he was a humble man. His legs, long and strong, covered in beige slacks that suited his calm demeanor, but not his climbing ability. And his hands. Oh, those hands that used to be slightly calloused after battle. Snow recalled rubbing them with soothing lotion in the late evening hours in her bedchamber. What she wouldn't give now to feel those calloused hands run up and down her body.

"Jack," she whispered and all the world melted away save for the two of them.

WHO'S THE BADDEST BITCH
OF ALL?

A ura stomped Snow's foot and snapped her out of the daydream. Snow cleared her throat. "I mean, Doctor Bean."

Jack tilted his head, his lips parted as if to say something, but Cindy interrupted.

"Can we get on with this please? I have shoes to try on."

The shoes were safely tucked away in Aura's closet, guarded by Beast. She had lured him into the room with a bone as large as a tree trunk, so Snow was certain the dog would be happily chomping away for a while.

Jack slapped his hands together. "Everyone, please take a seat."

They all filed further into the large room which resembled a gymnasium, complete with basketball hoops, balls of various sizes and colors, athletic mats, and the faint odor of gym socks. Each of the women chose a metal folding chair. They were arranged in a circle.

Jack settled into his own chair and Snow sat across from him, hoping distance would still her thumping heart.

Jack rested a clipboard on his lap, folded his hands and smiled at Snow.

"Now then, Miss White. What we do here is fairly simple and informal. In fact, you may call me Doc—everyone does." He removed his glasses. "This is a circle of trust." He swept his arms out across the space. "Whatever you say within this circle stays between us. Right ladies?"

Cindy rolled her eyes, Punzie snorted, and Bella yawned. Aura simply gave a nod.

Jack clicked his pen, frowning just a bit. "Yes, well. Whenever we have a newcomer such as yourself, we begin the session by telling what brought us here. Everyone participates in this exercise so we're all on the same playing field. So, Miss White, why don't we begin with you? Would you care to tell the group about the trouble you found yourself in that brought you to this point in your life?"

That was a loaded question if ever she had heard one. Good grief, if only she had the slightest idea what had brought her here—what had brought them all here—-or whom. Jack meant her crime, Snow knew, but she wasn't too enthusiastic about delving into that tale either.

She shuffled her feet. "Um... uh..." How could she tell Jack what she had done? She knew from their initial encounter that the details of her crime hadn't been disclosed to him. She was to reveal them in group. Now. Out loud. She shuddered at the thought. What would he think of her if he knew what she had done? Would he ever look at her the same way again? Trust her? Love her?

"Oh for fuck's sake." Cindy raised her perfectly manicured hand. "I'll go first, Princess." She stood up, straightening her pencil skirt and fluffing her hair. "After finding out that not only was my husband gay, but that he had been carrying on an affair with our driver, who happens to be my favorite employee, I got good and liquored up. Then I went to our house and cut out all the crotches from Trevor's underwear. Wrote, *I am a scum-sucking assface* on the backs of all his favorite shirts, then called his mother and told him her son was boinking the help." Cindy smiled at the memory. "That pissed her off more than the gay thing and the divorce." She buffed her nails on her skirt.

Jack shifted in his chair. "Go on, Cindy."

"Oh, right. So when Trevor got home, naturally he was upset and tried to deny everything, but I had proof. Someone had sent me pictures of the two of them."

Snow raised an eyebrow. Who would do such a thing? She wasn't exactly a fan of Cindy, at least not the Everafter version, but to send pictures of an affair seemed beyond cruel.

"So long story short, we got into an argument, someone called the cops, and just as I was about to knock Trevor on his ass, a policeman stepped in the way, took the punch, and well, here I am." She bowed.

Bella whistled, while Punzie and Aura clapped.

Cindy took a seat, crossed her arms and smiled at Jack.

Bella stood, the heels of her black boots scraping the floor. "My turn." She wore jeans and a white tank top with a button-down shirt over it. She slipped the shirt off and draped it over the back of her chair.

"As some of you know, I worked for what I thought was a perfectly respectable new and used bookstore."

This was news to Snow. She leaned forward, intrigued.

"So one day, after devoting close to a year to this sweet old man and his failing business. After him telling me I don't know how many times that I was the daughter he never had..." Her voice rose as she spoke. She began pacing, the heels of her boots stabbing the shiny wooden floor with every step. "After countless skipped lunches and a couple of pay cuts so he wouldn't lose the store, after talking about literature all hours of the day and night, thinking I had a great gig going, do you know what happened?" Bella stopped, folded her arms. Her question seemed to be directed at Snow.

"No," Snow said.

Bella gave her a wicked smile. "It was Monday and I was driving down Main Street on my way to open the bookstore. I had stopped to grab coffee first, one for me, one for Mr. Shithead. The weather was nice so the windows were down and the radio was playing a pop tune. I pulled up in front of the bookstore, and lo and behold, I saw a huge poster in the window of the place I considered my second home. The star of the poster was a mostly-naked woman with boobs bigger than my head, wearing a dog collar, tied to a fence, looking completely terrified while the man behind her leered."

Snow wrinkled her nose and inched back further in her seat, wishing there was a way to scrub that image from her mind. She shuddered.

Bella said, "I know, right?" She sighed, ran her fingers through her dark waves and climbed onto the back of her chair. She perched there for a moment, her feet on the seat. Her voice was full of disgust when she spoke again. "It was an advertisement for the new line of sleazy magazines he'd decided to sell to drum up business." She twisted her neck from side to side to look at the other women. "Now, I'm not a prude—I like erotica as much as the next chick, but I draw the line at a graphic publication titled "Sluts Who Need a Beating" with a centerfold that can only be described as a psychopath's idea of a good time."

Snow could feel Bella's pain. It practically leapt off her clothing and clamored around the room until it latched onto Snow. "What did you do?"

Bella shrugged. "The only thing I could do." She slid down and planted her backside firmly in the seat. She draped one bare arm across the chair back and said, "I put my foot on the gas and mowed down the storefront." She grinned and winked.

The grand gesture had never really been Bella's style. Snow couldn't help but be impressed. She also couldn't help but think it odd that Bella hadn't guessed her boss's true nature. She had a knack for reading people. At least, back home she had.

Punzie stretched and made a kind of cooing sound that turned into a full blown yawn. "Okay, I'll go next."

Bob hopped out of the pocket of her trench coat as she stood, and up onto the back of her chair. Open-toed stilettos peeked out from beneath the coat and Snow figured Punzie was probably working a double shift today.

Punzie said, "Being an exotic dancer is not an easy job. It's exhausting, mentally and physically. Some days, I put up with a lot of crap." She looked at Snow, a gleam in her eyes. "Some days, I don't." She wrapped her braid around her hand as if she were about to use it as a jump rope. "So a couple weeks ago this guy comes in one night and he's trying to distract me in the middle of my routine. He's snapping his fingers, waving at me, and just generally being a royal pain in the ass."

Jack's finger was propped on his temple, pen gently tapping his clipboard. He nodded.

Punzie wrapped her braid tighter around her wrist. "Then my favorite regular comes in and wouldn't you know it, he sits right next to the troublemaker. Naturally, I have to get close to him, so I shimmy on over there, open the micro shorts, and my regular inserts a bill. But before I can turn away, the asshole next to him jumps up and sticks his hand down my pants."

At this, Bob bounced on the chair, his bulging eyes glued

to Punzie and filled with fury. It struck Snow that in that moment something about the frog seemed familiar.

Punzie said, "I put that dickwad in a hair noose and banged his head on the stage a couple of times for good measure. Of course the cops didn't arrest *him* for assault, because hey, I'm a stripper, right?" She practically shouted that last part before her voice cracked and she lowered her head.

Snow felt a wave of sympathy for her former colleague. Of all the alternate lives of the five princesses in Everafter, Punzie's had to be the most grueling. The most degrading, too, she supposed. Snow hated to see her in such a state. She hated to see them *all* in such a state.

Whatever cruel fate or fiend has brought us to this, Snow vowed, *will pay and pay dearly.*

Punzie flipped her braid over her back and retied the belt on her coat before she sat down next to Bob. She absent-mindedly stroked his head, and he made a soft gurgling noise. "You know the funny thing is that he kept saying he was trying to 'save me.' From what, I don't know. A life of sin, I guess." Bob hopped into her lap and climbed up Punzie's shoulder. She giggled to herself. "Grim. Yep, he sure had a grim night."

Jack gave Punzie a questioning look.

She cocked her head. "Oh, didn't I tell you? That was the guy's name. Something Grimm."

Jack said, "That's odd. The report says his name was Story." He flipped through a few pages, stopped, and pushed his glasses further up the bridge of his nose. "Yes, here it is. Steve Story."

Jack removed his glasses and looked at Punzie for clarification.

Punzie shrugged. "Hmm. That's strange. I was sure he said his name was Grimm when I was shoving his face into the stage. Of course I could be wrong. It was pretty loud in there that night."

Snow shot Aura a look.

Aura's eyes widened.

The writer.

A HUNTING WE WILL SNOW

J ack noticed a look pass between Snow White and Aura Rose at the mention of the man named Grimm. Or Story. Whatever his name was. He thought that was curious, so he made a note of it.

Aura stood abruptly. "I'm a car thief."

She sat.

Jack set his pen down. "While I appreciate your enthusiasm to participate, Aura, I'm sure the rest of the group wouldn't mind if you cared to elaborate."

Aura looked at Bella. "You need more, Bookless?"

Bella was watching a spider weave a web around the water cooler. "I'm good."

"Hey, Cocktails. What about you?"

Cindy was applying pink lipstick that matched her top. "Nope."

"Princess?"

It took Snow a minute to realize that Aura was addressing her. "I'm fine, thanks."

"What about you, Pasties?"

166

"Bob and I are pretty bored with this whole show," Punzie said. "The sooner the grand finale, the better."

"See, Doc? They're all good."

Jack knew better than to push a patient into revealing more than she wanted to tell, so he decided not to press Aura. She seemed to be making progress and besides, after his last encounter with her at the diner, he suspected she might still be cross with him.

He readjusted his spectacles and said, "Well, I guess that just leaves you now, Miss White."

"Call me Snow."

Snow stood. She looked different than the last time he had seen her. More confident, but also...distant. She had seemed open, vulnerable just a few days before, but now she was even dressed differently. More casual.

What had changed?

Whatever it was, it suited her. She stood taller, her shoulders squared and her eyes determined. An enigma of bitter and sweet.

Jack wanted her all the more now.

He shook off the inappropriate thought and dug his pen into his thigh to remind him that it was highly unethical to think about a patient in such a manner.

But, oh, those red, red lips. What he wouldn't give to feel them on his own.

She cleared her throat and began. "I've had a sort of sixth sense when it comes to animals all my life. I can feel their emotions. Fear, pain, anger, joy, sorrow."

She reached for the water on the table behind her and took a sip.

"Sometimes they call to me." She glanced around the room. The other women seemed unusually alert. Intrigued, Jack suspected, to know more about this interesting creature. "They communicate with me through their emotions." She shook her head, her hair cascading across her shoulders. "I know it sounds crazy, but I can feel it."

Cindy scoffed, "Not at all, Snow. In fact, just the other day a pigeon told me he was tickled pink that Aura was off the streets because it left him more cars to shit on."

Punzie laughed and high-fived Cindy.

Aura growled.

Snow pursed her lips in annoyance. "May I finish?"

More confidence indeed, Jack thought.

Cindy put her hands up. "It's your funeral."

"Thank you." Snow took a deep breath. "I lived in a cottage in the woods just on the outskirts of town," She bit her lip and her face darkened. "One night, a doe visited my house. She had a bullet wound, which I treated and dressed. She drank, fed, and finally rested on a bed I made for her in my yard."

Aura sat a bit straighter in her seat. Bella too.

"The next morning, when I came out to check on her, she had been decapitated."

Punzie gasped.

Cindy said, "Ew."

Snow nodded. "I couldn't understand it. Whoever did it took only the head. A hunter would take the meat."

Jack nodded, his stomach queasy.

"Then, several days later, I saw the strangest thing. A hawk was up in a tree. It had just caught a field mouse from the look of the bulge in its neck, but when I got closer, I noticed it was missing its beak. And..." She looked away, gave a gentle shake of her head.

"And what?" Jack asked softly, his voice barely a whisper. He was enraptured by her story.

"And it had the feet of a rabbit."

Gasps from all around the room.

Snow took another drink of water. Jack wanted to reach

out and draw her to him—tell her she didn't have to go on, that the rest of the story didn't matter. She was safe here, with him. Until she had spoken, he hadn't thought what he had read in the report possible.

But he knew as she stood there, anger in her eyes, a tremble in her lips, that Snow White wasn't capable of saying anything but the whole truth.

"That afternoon, another deer came—a buck—beckoning me into the woods. Something about his eyes." She looked straight at Jack. "That's how it works, I guess. You can read a lot from a creature by looking into its eyes."

There was a rumble in Jack's gut that ran straight to his heart and camped there. Almost as if what she was saying was directed not just at him, but at his very soul.

He nodded.

"I followed him into the woods. Deeper and deeper we went until the trees grew so thick I thought I'd never find my way out."

She ran her slender fingers through her ebony hair. Took a breath.

A hush had fallen over the room. Even Cindy was quiet.

"The buck kept going, moving faster and faster and I was keeping pace behind him until we came upon an opening in the canopy. Just beyond was a field. He nudged me on, and as we looked down into the valley, I saw a warehouse." She took another sip of water. Paused. "I felt the fear first—felt it through my veins. Then I heard the screams."

Aura was staring at Snow with wide, unblinking eyes. Bella sat with her mouth hanging open and Cindy was scrunched up into her seat as if trying to disappear.

Snow lowered her head. "I won't tell you anymore about the experiments or the man behind them. I *will* tell you that only one of us walked out alive. The judge declared it involuntary manslaughter, although I wasn't the one who slaughtered him. I *was* the one, however, who freed the animals that did." She lifted her eyes. "The fire, I believe, was my only crime." Brought her gaze to Jack. "But I'm not sorry."

Jack was stunned. None of those details—about the animals, the experiments—had been included in the report the judge had given him on Snow. Her town, her rules. But these were important details, if he were to treat her properly. So why omit them?

He held Snow's stare and said, "I wouldn't be either."

Punzie cradled her frog. "No way. You're fucking with us, right?"

Snow just looked at her for a moment. Then she sat down, her face expressionless.

JACK THE GIANT SLAYER

The rest of the session included a lot of back-and-forth talk between Jack and the five princesses. He used words like "validation" when they tossed insults at each other, told them they needed to face what made them anxious and not to use the word "fear" because it fed their weaknesses. He played a film about two women on a cross country road trip, pausing the screen every so often to discuss the actions of the characters. Snow hardly saw a scene of it. She couldn't pull her eyes away from Jack.

SHE RECALLED the first time she saw him in Enchantment. They had been facing an ogre problem of epic proportions. As a leader, Snow had always tried to settle disputes with peace and fairness. Under her rule, there had only been one war—the War of the Five Crowns. That treacherous battle had inspired the blood treaty, drafted by Grimm, that would eventually unify the kingdoms. Peace reigned for years after they had all signed it. Until the ogres came.

General Gretel called an emergency session one morning.

Ogres had overtaken the south kingdom, Punzie's domain. Her army could no longer hold them back, and they swept through the land, pillaging, robbing, and beheading her people. Snow, Aura, Bella, and Cindy had sent troops, but they were no match for the ruthless giants. That was when Gretel first told them about Jack the Giant Slayer. Rumors of his reputation as a warrior were whispered in certain circles, and Gretel had called him in to meet the heads of state in the central castle of the kingdoms.

He entered the palace court looking gallant in battle garb, his leg muscles bulging beneath fitted pants, tunic untied at the chest, revealing a trace of dark hair beneath. He was tall —over six feet—with a wave of cocoa-colored hair and eyes the brilliant blue of the sea. His sword was sheathed as he bowed before Snow. She offered her hand and he shook it instead of kissing it—a sign that he respected women in power. They asked about his credentials, and he offered stories of battles waged and won, villages saved, lives spared, all in swift time. Jack explained that his father had handed his skills down to him when he was just a boy. Like Jack, he'd had a gift for destroying monsters.

Aura asked if his father would be joining him in battling the ogres and he said, "Aye. In spirit. He's away with the angels now, I'm afraid."

Snow's heart tugged at this, for he looked so forlorn as he said it.

Bella said, "Brothers, then?"

Jack shook his head. "I'm afraid not."

Punzie and Cindy exchanged a look. Punzie asked, "Is there no one else in your family with these gifts you claim?"

Jack smiled. "Just me mum, but I'm afraid she's too frail for war these days."

Snow smiled at Jack. She liked his confidence, his enthusiasm, and the fire in his eyes. He smiled back, scratched the stubble on his chin and folded his arms behind his back, waiting for the next question.

Cindy stood, "Excuse me, Mr...?"

"Just Jack, your majesty. I don't put on airs." His voice was like a saxophone, all sultry and melodious.

Cindy said, "Fine. Just Jack it is. Would you excuse us? We need to have a word in private, Just Jack."

Jack raised his eyebrows and looked around the room. It was yards long, so he opted to scoot all the way back towards the massive gilded double doors.

Cindy said, "Huddle, ladies."

The five of them formed a circle.

Cindy said, "Am I supposed to believe that this one jacknut is going to kill a whole army of ogres?"

Snow stuck her head out of the circle. She caught a glimpse of Jack's backside. It was just as delicious as the rest of him. "He appears strong enough. Tall. Muscular," she said.

Punzie slapped the back of Snow's head. "Would you turn off the bedroom eyes, Snow? We're looking for a soldier, not a concubine."

"You hit me again, Punzie, and I will feed that crown of yours through an orifice not meant for food intake."

Aura said, "Punzie's right, Snow, you're thinking with your hoochie."

"That's absurd." Snow said, smoothing out her gown. "And vulgar."

Cindy said, "But true. You sat there with your tongue hanging out of your mouth the whole time he was talking. It was embarrassing."

Bella squeezed the nearest ears she could reach, Punzie's and Aura's. "Will you bitches shut up and focus? Gretel recommended him, so I say he must have some skill. He must know what he's doing."

"Ahem, your majesties, might I suggest a demonstration?" Jack called.

Snow's face grew unbearably hot. "I swear, if he heard any of you…" she whispered through gritted teeth.

They all stood and turned to face Jack.

Snow said, "That's a lovely idea, Jack. Please do."

Cindy said, "So what, we're going to call in an ogre?"

Bella glared at her. "Let the man finish."

Jack bowed. "With permission. I'd like to demonstrate on the chandelier and…" He completed a 360 degree turn and pointed up to the fifty foot ceiling behind them. "And that clock, which, if I may be frank, will be destroyed."

Punzie shrugged. "Knock yourself out, Just Jack."

Bella turned to her. "Seriously?"

Punzie slid her eyes to Bella. "What? I always hated that clock. I feel like its staring at me."

"Do we all agree?" Bella asked and the others nodded.

Jack sprang into action. He unsnapped a compartment on his leather belt, liberated a dagger and stuck the blade between his teeth as he catapulted off the ground, bounced off the far wall like a rubber ball, and leapt onto the chandelier. Gripping the frame with both hands, he pumped his legs, swung himself once, twice, and on the third push darted through the air with a warrior cry. He pulled the knife from his teeth and plunged it into the center of the clock. His feet smacked the wall with such force, that he dove, then rebounded backward, tucking his knees into his chest. He somersaulted through the air and landed on his feet.

The women all stood still and speechless for several moments, which was a rarity.

Then Snow gave Jack a boisterous ovation. "Bravo!" She whistled. "Bravo!"

Bella tugged Snow by the skirt of her gown. "Pull it together, Princess," she hissed.

To Jack, Bella said, "Explain how that tiny dagger can kill an ogre?"

Jack approached the stage where the thrones were situated. "It can't actually. You see the beanoppus of the ogre—that's the part of his brain that causes his violent tendencies—lies directly behind his right eye. If he's injured there, it destroys that part of him that is compelled to maim and destroy."

"And?" Aura said.

"And then he can be rehabilitated into a productive member of society." Jack smiled.

Cindy blew out a sigh and stepped forward. "Okay, Just Jack. Thank you for your time, but I think we'll seek assistance elsewhere."

"Wait—" Jack said.

Punzie said, "I agree with Cindy. The only good ogre is a dead ogre." She took her place at her throne.

Snow moved to stand behind her own throne. She thought her blood oath sisters were being too hasty, but they did have a point. She had seen what the ogres were capable of, and it was the stuff of nightmares. "What if you *must* kill one? Surely, they cannot all be changed. Blood begets blood, does it not?"

"Aye," Jack said. "Not all can be saved. In that case, the only way to kill one..." He sprinted to the other side of the room, leapt to the top of a white balcony and sprang toward the chandelier. He unsheathed his sword and with one mighty swoop, sliced the chain clean through. It crashed to the ground in a spray of glass beads and glass fragments as he jackknifed through the air, landing near the thrones. "...is to cut the head off."

He pulled a tiny green bag from his pocket and tossed it onto the smashed fixture. A web of thick, gnarled vines grew from it and roped the broken pieces of crystal together, crushing them into itself and dissolving every last piece. Then the entire clumpy mess melted into the floor.

The five women stared in awe at the empty space where the chandelier had met its demise.

Bella said, "First, you're going to pay for that. Second," she looked at the others and they all nodded vigorously. "You're hired."

It wasn't long after that day that Jack earned a permanent position in the royal army. And a permanent place in Snow's bed.

Now, as she watched him flip the lights on and gather his notes and clipboard, she was heartbroken that he didn't even recognize her.

How cruel life could be, she thought.

THIS MAGIC MOMENT

Bella stopped to use the restroom and Cindy rushed out of the building to have a cigarette. Punzie followed her. Aura pulled Snow aside and said, "How you doing?"

"Fine."

Something on her face must have told Aura that Snow was anything but fine. "Bullshit. I know how you feel about Jack."

Snow shrugged. "There's nothing I can do about it, so let's just figure out this mess we're in, form a plan, and get out of this forsaken town."

Aura said, "We have to tell them, you know."

Snow looked at Aura. "Tell them what?"

"About Granny," Aura snapped.

"Oh, yes, right. So we tell them, then we find Granny, then we get answers. Are we going to the café?"

"That's usually the plan."

"Okay." Snow squared her shoulders, took a deep breath, and walked toward the doors. "Let's do this."

Snow wished Bella had found her story element before

Cindy had. Snow wanted Bella back so very badly because Bella was the voice of reason and respected here in Everafter. The captain of this ship of fools. If anyone could convince Punzie and Cindy who they really were and what needed to be done to get home, it was Bella.

The crystal shoes were tucked away for now, but eventually Cindy would go looking for them. Snow was going to have to convince her to touch them with both hands before slipping them on her feet. No easy task, to be sure, because Cindy loved shoes like Bella loved books. But if Cindy stepped into the famous slippers, that would be her downfall, the same as if Snow had bitten the apple, or if Aura had pricked her finger on the spinning wheel. All of them were vulnerable to the objects that had harmed them in their original stories.

As Snow and Aura waited outside the restroom for Bella, Snow thought about the insurance policy she had stashed away in case the others never discovered their artifacts. She felt magic when she had touched that apple, and certainly it had been infused with it somehow, because how else would it have transported her so completely back to her true self? She thought that maybe, if they didn't find all the pieces they needed to remind the princesses of who they really were, then the apples could help retrieve the other lost memories. That's why she had asked Aura to pick exactly five and hide them away for safe keeping.

The mirrors, or rather, the places where mirrors usually hung—on the bathroom wall and again in the grand upper ballroom—seemed to also contain a hint of magic, although Snow wasn't privy to how they functioned. Unless...could it be the house itself was enchanted?

She thought about the 'no mirrors' rule, wondered why she hadn't found any on her search of the house even tucked away in a forbidden closet. As ruler of her kingdom, she had

had her own magic mirror for a time. It was now painted entirely black and safely stowed away back in Enchantment. She had ordered it destroyed after it had been used against her once, but her advisors warned that destroying it would be a mistake. That its power was unbound and immeasurable and that there was no telling the repercussions of shattering it. Threads of many lives could have been altered. And she wasn't about to let that happen a second time. So the silver was glazed over to stifle the magic and to prevent anyone from using its powers for evil.

Snow thought again about the rooms she had explored. The clocks, the clothes, the trinkets, and that baffling locked door that she hadn't been able to gain access to. What did it contain?

The more she thought about it, the more she considered Aura's conviction that Granny had been taken against her will by someone who meant them all harm could be accurate. Snow wanted to believe that Granny really was on their side.

Unless...the rooms were locked. Or marked 'Do Not Enter'. So was she really collecting those things to jog their memories? Or did she do it to block them? Or, more worrisome, did she squirrel away those objects to hide them from someone else? Someone dangerous? Did those thrift sale finds contain magic? Or was Granny mad?

There was no way to be certain. Not until they located the old woman.

Bella exited the restroom and the three of them pushed through the glass doors of the community center and stepped out beneath a stifling sky.

"What have you bitches been doing? Braiding each other's hair?" Punzie said. "I've only got an hour before my shift, and if I'm late, the DJ plays his own list. Do you know how hard it is to make *Build Me Up Buttercup* look sexy with a bum ankle?"

"Sorry," Snow mumbled, wondering what kind of clientele went to strip clubs in the middle of the day. Homeless guys? Men who lived with their mothers? Mental patients?

The five of them walked the three blocks to Gretel's Café, chattering about Snow's story and taking bets on the authenticity of it.

"Admit it, you made that up just so we'd think you had some boulders between your legs," Punzie said.

"Guess you'll never know," said Snow.

Cindy complained about the humidity the entire way. "I swear, my make-up is going to slide right off my face," she said.

Aura rolled her eyes and Punzie said, "Try walking in six inch heels with a thong up your crack, Miss Priss, then we'll talk."

Gretel's Café was a quaint, curtained establishment with a row of blue leather booths lining one wall, wooden tables in the center, and a long Formica bar where the waitresses served hot coffee and cold sodas. The kitchen was behind the bar, and Snow could see two cooks in white paper hats bustling over the stainless steel pass.

They chose a table in a quiet corner. Gretel greeted them immediately with, "Hey convicts, what's shaking? Kill anyone today?"

Snow's four housemates looked at her and shifted uncomfortably.

She looked directly into Gretel's eyes, smiled, and said, in a deadpan tone. "The day isn't over yet."

Aura grimaced and Snow realized that she had slipped out of her unassuming, demure Everafter persona. That was probably not a good idea. At least not yet.

Gretel stared at Snow for a beat, not sure how to respond. Punzie put her hands under her chin and Cindy mimicked her, batting her lashes at Gretel.

"That's right, fry girl, there's a new bad bitch in town."

Punzie looked around, cupped her hand around her mouth and in a loud whisper, said, "What this chick did makes me look like a Girl Scout."

Gretel swallowed hard, tossed some menus on the table and hurried off.

Snow was smiling when she turned back to face her roommates, who were all giggling.

All but one.

Bella's face was ice.

I SPY WITH MY FAE EYE

Tink had never considered her small stature to be an advantage. For one thing, she couldn't watch a movie in an actual theater because inevitably someone would sit directly in front of her obstructing her view. She also had trouble reaching the pedals of any normal sized automobile because she needed a booster seat just to see over the steering wheel, and—most infuriating—people tended not to take a person seriously who couldn't hop onto a bar stool without the aid of a pogo stick.

However, as she sat in a corner booth at Gretel's Café, Tink realized that being a small person was perfect for spying in a restaurant, because (a.) she could hide behind the giant menu and (b.) she could slip into a bathroom like a whisper and comfortably crouch on top of a toilet seat undetected like she was doing right now.

She had been at the café for half an hour and hadn't heard a lot of the women's conversation. While Tink's hearing was superior, she had a difficult time filtering out background noise. She hadn't anticipated just how much background noise littered a busy restaurant until she was at the mercy of it. The whir of a blender, the obnoxious cackle of teenagers, the constant chime of bells, waitresses rattling off the specials, the telephone—all of these noises penetrated Tink's delicate ears, making it difficult to eavesdrop. So when two of the parolees rose to head for the restroom, Tink dashed in ahead of them low and fast like a rat terrier.

After a minute, Cindy's obnoxious perfume was slapping at Tink's nose and she had to pinch it to keep from sneezing.

"So the old bat didn't come home, big deal. Maybe she's on a bender," the blonde said.

Aura responded in a scratchy voice that grated on Tink's nerves. "I don't think so, Cindy. I think something might be wrong."

Tink realized they were talking about their housemother, Granny.

Her ears pricked with interest. If Granny wasn't supervising the house, what would the judge do? Would she arrange for an alternative living situation? Or would she appoint a new den mother? Someone who would keep her eyes and ears glued to the situation, perhaps. Someone who might even find violations that would send that awful Aura back to the slammer. And maybe even Snow White.

Tink didn't like the way Doctor Bean looked at the dark haired beauty during the session she had just spied on. She didn't like it one bit. Of course, she only caught brief glimpses of his adoring gaze while she was jumping outside the window of the gymnasium at the community center, but still. It made her angry.

And oh, what she wouldn't give to get out of the judge's house and away from that horrible wolf.

She was so elated at the thought that she let out a tiny squeal.

Aura said, "Who's there?"

Tink held her breath as she heard the soft click of heels approach the stalls.

The clicking stopped and Tink saw the top of Aura's head poke beneath the stall door. She scrambled on top of the toilet tank and pressed herself to the wall.

Cindy said, "What the hell are you doing?" A door opened and closed. A lock slid into place.

"I thought I heard something," said Aura.

"So you're going to poke your head underneath the stalls like a pervert. Oh, and speaking of crimes, I found my shoes in your closet, you whore."

Aura's head vanished. "You did?" Her voice faded just a bit and Tink heard another stall door open.

Shoes? What shoes? Tink wondered. The judge ordered Cindy to donate all her shoes.

"Yes I did, you klepto. Did you think you'd get away with it?"

"Calm down, Cindy...um..." Aura stammered. Quickly she added, "You asked me to hang onto them, remember?"

Cindy's tone faltered. "I did? That doesn't sound like me."

"Yes, the other night."

"Now why the hell would I do that? Those things are worth more than your whole *life*."

A flush.

Valuable shoes? Tink was thrilled at this. She would have a violation on Cindy now and the judge would be so pleased with her impeccable detecting. She was *way* better at this than that stupid oaf, Robin.

"I don't know. You said something about Granny finding them."

A zipping sound and another flush.

"I did?" Cindy didn't sound certain.

"Yep. You were pretty liquored up."

"*That* sounds like me."

Liquor? That was another violation of Cindy's probation. Tink clamped a hand over her mouth to keep from shouting with joy.

"Did you try them on?" Aura asked, her voice shaking a bit. A faucet turned on and Tink had to strain to hear the rest.

"Not yet. I saw a dress at a boutique that would go perfectly with them and I wanted to try the whole ensemble on at the same time."

"Maybe you could model for us later."

"Don't be weird."

The faucet stopped gushing, and a hand dryer howled to life.

After they washed and dried, Aura said, "Come on, I have to get to my service."

The door opened and closed and Tink waited a few beats before exiting the stall.

She pulled out her tiny recorder and spoke into it, kicking herself for forgetting to turn it on when she had first snuck into the bathroom. "Tink's spy notes, volume two."

Tink made a record of the conversation she had heard between Aura and Cindy, flipped off the recorder, and stepped out of the restroom. She hurried out of the café. She would call the judge as soon as she got to her car.

DESPERATE JUDGES

J udge Redhood was growing desperate, and she wasn't happy about it. Desperate people do desperate things, and she had already done something so drastic even *she* couldn't believe it. The judge did not like plot twists, especially in a plan of her own creation. Well, mostly her creation. She wasn't the headliner of this operation—more like the emcee. One who had just thrown a monkey wrench into her own lineup, but what choice did she have? She couldn't very well let things escalate, though she suspected they already had. There was no proof —yet—but she was going to get to the bottom of whatever was going on even if it killed her. Or someone else, preferably.

It had taken nearly a year to get to this point. A year of strategic planning, careful crafting, arranging all the players just so. Not to mention developing not only the perfect spell, but the perfect cloak to veil the spell. It was brilliant, really. The effects of her magic, well, *their* magic, was like nothing she had ever seen before. She was so proud of herself.

Until of course she was betrayed. *Again.* The thought of it made her blood boil. She picked up a golf club that was leaning up against her desk and smacked a glass lamp with it. The lamp flew to the far wall and shattered into tiny pieces, leaving a modest dent to match the others.

Fang came rushing around the corner, jaws dripping with saliva. He growled at the shattered lamp, head low, hackles poking the air.

"Nothing to worry about, my pet. Mommy was just unleashing a bit of frustration." She blew out a deep breath, feeling a bit more in control of her emotions. She would need that control for what she was about to do. She couldn't go off half-cocked. Not now. There was too much at stake. She had come too far.

The judge smoothed her navy fitted jacket over her matching slim skirt and fluffed her fiery hair. Her phone was on her desk, and she picked it up and, slipped it into her pocket next to the key. Then she climbed the stairs to the second level of her woodland estate.

She wasn't certain how long the curse was going to cling to its targets, but she could feel magic seeping into this land through the seams.

So who had brought it? And more importantly—did the princesses have any? She hoped Tink would provide some answers. Robin had been of no help at all, the useless toad. Tink should have been following those bitches all morning. Hopefully the girl would arrive any moment with a report, and hopefully it would give the judge just cause to lock one of them up again. Separately, they would be much easier to control, and the magic—if it *had* found them here—would dissipate.

She shook her head at the notion that *they* had found each other in Everafter. Oh, she'd had no doubt that four of them would wind up standing before her bench at one point or another. They were spoiled rotten princesses, after all, with everything handed to them on a silver platter most of their vapid lives. But that they came through the courtroom in succession and in the same timeframe baffled her. She had no explanation for it, but she would soon. Even if she had to use the threat of Fang himself to get some answers, she would have them.

It was Snow White's crime that really had her stymied.

Pure of heart, innocent, doe-eyed Snow White had been such a goody two-shoes as long as she had known her that she was still dumbfounded by her actions. Perhaps, the judge thought as she unlocked the door that led to the third floor of the house, the spell had been even more powerful than she'd thought. Perhaps it had tamped down their true selves so deep that they would never recover their memories. Or their crowns.

"And wouldn't that be delicious." A smile spread across her face.

As she ascended the final stairs, the judge reached into her pocket and pulled out her mobile phone. She had purchased one for Tink, but the careless girl often forgot to carry it with her. Still, she'd try to reach her. See if she had uncovered any wrongdoing. It rang five times before she hung up.

The door at the end of the dark hallway loomed before her and the judge stopped. She hesitated, contemplating her next move. She needed answers, sure, but how far was she willing to go to get them? She needed to secure the town of Everafter, too. But was she prepared to risk her own happiness to do it?

The key was in her pocket, and she could smell Fang's earthy scent trailing down the hall behind her. He must have followed her up the stairs. She found his steady breath comforting, the rhythm of his heartbeat soothing. A calmness washed over her. There was something about Fang's sheer survival instinct that penetrated her very soul. She gathered strength from the wolf, inhaling it into her lungs.

"There is only so much magic stored here," she said to herself. "Do what must be done."

She still hadn't decided how to rectify her predicament, nor had she come to any light-bulb realization of the best action course. All she knew was that she had to do something soon. She couldn't let them remember, couldn't allow the princesses to gain control. Or it would be *her* head on a platter.

The phone rang in her hand and the judge jumped.

She looked at the number and groaned. She'd been dreading this call, fearing it even, but she had proven her loyalty time and again and she would continue to do so.

She answered the call with, "Everything is under control."

She waited for instructions. Then she plucked the key from her pocket, slipped it into the lock and entered the room that she alone knew existed.

A TRAIL OF GLITTER

S now looked up from her spinach salad just in time to
see a trail of glitter flash down the hall toward the
restaurant's bathroom before it dissipated. She didn't
think much of it until she recalled what the pixie had said
about taking Robin Hood's place.

She made mention of this to Bella and Punzie who
laughed so hard at the absurdity of the tiny girl acting as
their parole officer that Snow was afraid one of them might
choke.

Upon returning from the restroom, Aura didn't find it so
amusing. "I think we need to stage an ambush."

Punzie said, "Don't tell me you're afraid of that little
gnat." She popped a fry in her mouth.

Aura said, "No, but I am afraid of what her boss could do
to us." She glanced at each of her housemates.

Bella stood. "She's right." She dropped some money on
the table. "Let's roll."

The five of them waited just around the corner and lo and
behold, after a few minutes, they spotted Tink skipping

down the sidewalk holding a recorder in her dainty hands and giggling.

Bella rounded the corner first. "Well, well. If it isn't the fly on the wall."

Tink shoved the recorder in her pocket, jutted her lip out, and said, "Leave me alone."

"Bzzzt! Try again," Cindy said.

Tink glared at all of them as they formed a circle around her. "I'm not afraid of you. Any of you."

Bella stepped forward. "You should be." She gestured behind her where Snow stood outside the circle. "You see, Snow White back there wanted to take a crack at you, but she's already killed once, and any more than that in a month is just bad form."

Tink slid a fearful gaze to Snow White, who sighed.

Bella crossed her arms and said, "But I drew the short stick. So to speak."

"Oh, a short joke. Very original," Tink said. Her voice was steady but Snow saw the sprite quiver.

"Bella, please, let's not make it worse." Snow stepped forward. "Look, Tink, we know what you're up to, but it's not polite to eavesdrop on people's private conversations. So why don't you just give us the recording and we can all be on our merry way."

Punzie looked at her watch. "Can we speed this along? If DJ Ray takes his break before I get there, he plays the jukebox and every damn record skips. *If I Can Turn Back Time* is repetitive enough, believe me."

Cindy said to Tink, "Listen, you little moth. Whatever you think you heard, you don't know the whole story. So just give us the tape and we can forget all about it. There's no need to report any of this to the judge."

Tink backed away and shook her head. "You can't take my property. That's illegal."

Bella said, "I'm pretty sure it's illegal to record a bathroom conversation too."

"Not to mention throwing a rock at a windshield," said Snow.

"And assaulting a peace officer," said Aura.

Tink chewed her bottom lip. She swung her head from left to right and scanned the group.

"But, that was all in the line of duty." Her hands were stuffed tightly in the pockets of her pastel-colored dress.

Bella tapped her foot. "I don't think the judge would see it that way."

"She's pretty much a stickler for the law," said Aura.

Cindy snorted. "Yeah. Just look at us."

Snow said, "You don't want to be like us, do you Tink?"

Something shifted in Tink's eyes, and a slow smiled spread across her face. She bit her lip.

Snow cocked her head and looked at Aura. Aura's brow was wrinkled at first, and then, something seemed to dawn on her. She crossed her arms. "Or maybe you do."

Tink vehemently shook her head. "No! No I don't."

Aura stepped forward. "Oh yes. I've seen the way you look at Doc. You want to spend more time with him, don't you?"

Snow snapped her head to Aura. What was she up to?

Punzie said, "Oh yeah? No problem. What about you give us the tape and don't say anything to the judge about what you may have heard and we'll set you up on a date with Dr. Feel-good?"

"No!" said Snow.

They all looked at her. Aura reached over and pinched her.

"Ow. I mean, how? How would we do that?" Snow said.

Tink's eyes widened and her ears twitched.

Punzie said, "No problem. I'll take care of it."

"So is it a deal?" Cindy asked.

Tink looked at Punzie, her eyes full of hope. Then she seemed to think better of the idea and shook her head. "No. No deal. I have integrity, and that's what Jack respects. I'll win him all on my own." She straightened her spine. "And you should be concerned about your housemother. What have you done with her?" The little sprite narrowed her eyes and flared her nostrils.

Bella ran a hand through her chestnut hair. "Plan B it is then."

"W-what's plan B?" Tink asked.

Bella stepped forward and put her hands on Tink's shoulders. "Plan B is we stuff you in the trunk of my car, drive you up to the canyon and feed you to the coyotes."

At this point, Snow would have stepped in, but something about the pixie's crush on her love had scrambled her brain momentarily. She stood there, waiting for the scene to play out.

"You wouldn't dare," Tink said defiantly.

Bella pulled out a roll of duct tape, and faster than a blink she hog tied the Pixie right there in the alley behind the restaurant.

That snapped Snow out of her trance. She pulled Bella aside and said, "You're not really going to stuff her in the trunk of your car, are you?"

Bella whispered out of the corner of her mouth, "Relax, Princess. I'm reading to some wayward kids today at the juvie home. I'm going to spike her slushy or whatever the hell she drinks, and stick her in a classroom. She'll blend right in, and by the time it wears off I'll have the recorder and she won't remember a thing." She looked at Tink squirming on the ground like an overturned beetle. "Who knows, maybe she'll learn something."

"I think that plan needs work."

"Do you have a better idea? Because I'm not going to take another strike. I have no idea how long she's been doing the Devil's dirty work, or what she may have on me, but my time in Hell House is almost up and I don't plan on sticking around this dump of a town after that."

Punzie said, "Well I'd love to stay and help, but I don't want to." She and Bob shuffled off to the club.

Snow tapped her foot. She needed to tell Bella what was going on, but without the book, she suspected Bella wouldn't believe her.

Wait—

"Did you say you were reading to children?"

"That's my assignment today. Why?"

What if she stumbled across the book? What if she read it? That would be horrible. But how could Snow stop her?

"Is there a specific story you have in mind?"

Bella shrugged. "They seem to like vampire stories. Couldn't keep them on the shelves when I worked for that pervert. Thought I'd go with that." She narrowed her eyes. "Why?"

Why indeed. "Just curious."

Bella gave Snow a dubious look.

Snow tried to sound chipper. "A bit of advice. Stay away from fairytales. Kids hate those things. Especially anthologies."

"How the hell would you know?" Bella crossed her arms.

"Oh, um, I..."

Aura stepped in then. "I saw those books in your car, Bella. I borrowed one if that's all right. An old lady on my route mentioned she wanted something to read next time I dropped off her meal."

Bella looked from Aura to Snow. Snow blinked at her and Aura smiled.

Bella wagged her finger at them. "I don't know what the

fuck is going on with you nutjobs, but when we're done with our community crap, the three of us are going to have a chat."

Snow shrugged. "Nothing's going on."

Aura scoffed. "Of course not."

Bella eyed them suspiciously. "Yeah, right. Help me get this dragonfly into the car."

Tink writhed on the ground, attempting to scream as Cindy tried to stifle her with whiskey. It sloshed all over the fairy's dress.

Bella turned around and slapped the bottle from Cindy's hand. "You dipshit, I can't slip her into the school if she reeks like a distillery."

Aura tapped Snow's shoulder. She winked and mouthed *the book*.

Snow flashed her eyes to Bella and gave a slight nod. Aura nodded back and Snow almost cheered. She had found Bella's story nemesis.

All they needed now was Punzie's. And then, maybe they could work together to find a way home.

YOU CAN'T TAKE THE HOOD OUT OF ROBIN

After Robin made certain the women had entered the community center to attend their group therapy sessions, he circled back around to Granny's house. The session would last at least an hour and after that they usually grabbed a bite at Gretel's, giving Robin plenty of time to investigate. That's what he told himself he was doing anyway. Investigating.

Robin hadn't committed a crime since he was a boy, and even then he'd considered his acts of thievery a kind of social service. He believed it profoundly unfair that some had so very much while others had little to nothing. Especially when those with nothing dedicated their lives to building the wealth of others. He learned too, simply by observing their behavior, that the rich and prosperous rarely appreciated or even kept inventory of their possessions. So if a bakery shoppe was about to toss out its two-day-old bread, what harm would it do to intercept that bread and deliver it to a single mother raising four children? Or if the banker had sixteen jackets and only wore three of them, why not take the others and pass them out to the men who tended the fields in rags?

As Robin stood at the back door of Granny's house picking the lock, he couldn't help but think that those memories seemed like a lifetime ago. A world away. So far away in fact, he could hardly recall the names or the faces of the compatriots who had joined his cause. He wondered, as the tumblers shifted and clicked in the lock and the door yawned open, if his old friends knew he was a lawman now.

Or rather, had been a lawman. He didn't know what he should call himself anymore. Maybe he would open a private practice. Robin Hood, P.I. That had a nice ring to it. Marion could mind the phones, perhaps do the technological detecting that Robin wasn't very skilled at. Yes, he thought, maybe that's exactly what they should do. He would run the idea by Marion as soon as he drummed up the nerve to tell her he had gotten fired.

It wasn't that he was afraid of how she might react to him when he delivered the news. She loved Robin, supported him no matter what, and he her. It was that Robin feared Marion would get herself in trouble by unleashing her temper on the judge. How many times had he heard her say, "I do not like that woman!"

Robin Hood adjusted his hat as he scanned Granny's spacious, drab kitchen. He had never been in this room, so he thought he may as well start here. It was surprisingly clean. Not a dirty dish in sight, and there were fresh flowers on the table, which he found odd but endearing. It put a smile on his face. Perhaps Granny's girls weren't as callous as they pretended to be.

He began his search by opening cabinets and drawers, sifting through the pantry, the refrigerator, even the stove. Truth be told, he had no idea what he was looking for, but something strange was going on in this town and it all seemed to center around this house. Or at the very least, around the women beneath its roof. Questions had been swarming his mind ever since the judge had assigned these women to Robin's caseload. And even more so since she had fired him for...for what anyway? Not finding any more charges to slap on them? That made no sense. It was almost as if she didn't want them to succeed. As if she was determined to lock the women up forever.

As he made his way into the hall and toward a room marked "Do Not Enter," Robin wondered for the second time that day where Granny had gotten off to. It wasn't like her to leave the house too often except for Saturdays and Sundays, and even then she'd only take a few short hours to satiate her shopping urges. He hoped she was all right. Perhaps he should pop into her favorite haunts, ask if anyone had seen her. She was elderly after all—she could have gotten confused or fallen ill.

Robin checked the handle on the door labeled "Do Not Enter" and discovered it wasn't locked. It was a small space, so he had to scrunch down so his head wouldn't smack the ceiling. He flipped on a light and found himself surrounded by dusty ball gowns, tiaras, slippers, and other garments best left to storage or a costume shoppe. He sighed and closed the door behind him.

Robin wound through the bookless library next, and his thoughts turned to Bella. It seemed strange to him that a lover of literature like her boss, Harvey, would transform his little bookstore into a vulgar peepshow. He almost felt sorry for Bella, but she'd broken the law and she had to face the consequences.

And now you've broken it too, he reminded himself.

He searched the dining room, carefully listening for any sign of Granny or the women. There was nothing suspicious there, either—just formal china, antique furniture, and dusty old rugs. The next door he came across was also marked "Do Not Enter." This one was locked, so he used one of his tools from the old days to rectify the situation and found himself staring at a room filled with nothing but clocks, with numbers painted and pasted to the walls. He couldn't think of a reason for such a room to exist, except that Granny's brain may have gone around the bend. He shut the door and continued through to the parlor and the roll-top desk.

He rummaged through the drawers, glancing through timecards and files on the girls who'd stayed at Granny's house. He found several copies of Granny's rules, receipts, tax records, canceled checks, to-do lists for Hansel, chores lists, grocery lists, pens, notepads, paperclips, and the general junk that most people keep in their desks.

Back in his thieving days, Robin had learned that antique desks such as these often harbored secret compartments. They were cheaper than safes, and most thieves wouldn't think to break into a wooden desk. Occasionally, the wood-worker would install a separate storage caddy beneath the main drawer. Robin checked and found none. Another option was a fake backing that when removed, revealed several smaller compartments. He moved the desk away from the wall and tapped the back. Nothing there. A third trick was a second roller within the roll top. Robin reached his hand inside the desk, carefully holding the roll top down as far as he could with his other hand. He reached up and back, sliding his fingers along the inside of the rolling cover until they stumbled over something cold. Metal.

He fumbled around and found a simple brass fastener. No lock mechanism. With one twist, the second roller swooshed down from the inside and papers spilled onto the desk. Robin reached to pick them up when he heard the growl of a two-hundred pound canine behind him.

WHO'S BEEN SLEEPING IN MY BED?

T hree hours, eight dog walks, sixteen litter box changes, and a whole lot of furry love later, Snow White, ruler and mediator of the United Kingdoms of Enchantment and newest volunteer at the Everafter Animal Shelter was ready to take on the world. If only she knew where that world was located.

She sighed, said goodbye to her new friends, tied her hoodie around her waist and stepped out under a stormy sky. She smacked directly into Hansel on the sidewalk.

He was drinking something blue and eating something brown and they were now mushed together on his white shirt.

"Oh, Hansel, I'm so sorry. I didn't see you there," she said. She was wearing a silk scarf and she removed it to mop up the mess she had created.

Hansel simply stood there a moment grinning at her. "Hey, that's okay. It's not every day a gorgeous woman ravages my body." He discarded the remainder of his beverage and what must have been a muffin in a nearby trashcan. Then he sauntered back to her, put his hands to his sides, lifted his gaze to the sky and said, "Go to town."

Snow stepped back. "Very funny." She smirked at him. "And a bit pervy."

Hansel bowed. "My apologies, Madam. It shan't happen again." He reached for her hand and kissed it softly, his left arm twined around his back.

Snow was smiling until the moment his lips brushed her skin. When Hansel kissed her hand, something electric passed through Snow's very being. It rushed through every nerve and muscle in her body and sailed straight into her heart with a rollicking jolt. She felt it pulsate and her breathing intensified. Her blood pumped so rapidly she thought she might faint, but she caught herself and focused on slowing her breaths.

What was happening?

Hansel grabbed both of her arms to lend Snow support. "Whoa, easy there, Snow. I've got you."

His eyes were filled with concern, fear...even—was that caring? Snow shifted her gaze to the sidewalk. She didn't want to see what she was seeing, feel what she was feeling, this...passion. Not for Hansel. They'd only just met here in this world. And back home, he was simply a friend. The brother of her army leader.

Cindy's true love.

Snow watched a large ant gather the crumbs of the muffin Hansel had been eating before she smashed into him. It collected every last bit of food before scurrying off to meet up with its colony and enjoy the rest of its short life. She recalled reading somewhere that ants had memories—that soldiers could lead the rest of the army to food sources that would feed the queen.

She wondered, in horror, how many memories of her

own life she had lost since they had been catapulted into this land. What had happened to *her* colony? Her head was a swirl of meetings and moments in Everafter and Enchantment, all mixed together as if they'd been plopped into a blender and spat out with no rhyme or reason to their meaning or order.

No matter how deep she dug, she couldn't recover a single romantic tie between she and Hansel. And yet, his touch was familiar, his kiss, intimate. The way he smiled at her when he bent his head to read her face. How his golden eyes swirled with fireworks.

"Are you all right? Snow?"

At the sound of his voice, that word charged through her head again. *Betrayal.* At first, when she'd heard the word inside Granny's house, she'd thought it was a message sent to warn her, as a fairy godmother might, of impending danger. She realized now the word ran through her mind whenever Hansel was near. What was it he had said on the stairs of Granny's house? *Oh, you're a threat all right, Snow White. The kind of woman who inspires a man to slay a dragon, relinquish his throne, or fall on his sword for just one kiss.*

Snow felt her hands grow clammy and her stomach somersault as an alternative theory wormed through her thoughts. Were the whispers for *her*? Had *she* betrayed Jack?

How long had she been trapped here? What had happened back in Enchantment before this curse? What had she done there that she would forever regret?

The very notion made her ill, but she had to try it on for size. See if it fit.

"Seriously, Snow, say something or I'm going to pick you up and carry you straight to the hospital."

She slipped from Hansel's grip and backed away. "I'm sorry. It's the heat. I just got dizzy for a moment. I'm fine. Really."

She studied him, searching for a sign that they had been lovers, but her mind was too foggy now to focus.

Hansel didn't look convinced. "Let me walk you home at least. There's a few things I need to take care of over at Granny's anyway. I can make you something to eat and you can rest while I work. Then I'll check in on you after. Maybe we could watch a movie or something."

He reached for her again and she wrenched away as if she'd been burned.

Hansel's smile faltered. He scratched his head and stuffed his hands in his pockets. "Look, Snow, I was just joking earlier. I'm really not a creep."

Snow gave a shaky laugh that even she didn't believe. "I know that, Hansel. I just don't want either of us to get into trouble. You know. With Granny."

He pressed his lips together as if he knew that was a feeble excuse. Which, given all that Snow knew now, it was. But she couldn't very well tell him the truth. That she was in love with Jack and that once upon a time, Cindy had been his fiancée.

Good Heavens, what a mess they were all in.

"Hey, I get it. But I am going to walk you home. I just want to make sure you're safe."

She was just about to agree to that arrangement when she heard a horn blare, tires screech behind her and a drunken blonde shout, "Hey Gingersnap, step away from the convict. I repeat step away from the convict."

Snow and Hansel both turned to find Aura driving a car that didn't belong to her (or anyone in the house for that matter), Cindy sloshing liquor out the passenger window, and Punzie in the back seat—Bob perched on her shoulder—looking as if she was about to discard her lunch.

Snow turned to Hansel and shrugged. "I guess my chariot awaits."

Hansel saluted her. "Good luck with that."

She felt him watching as she climbed into the back seat, and as Aura punched the pedal, Snow stole one last look out the review window as the four of them darted into the setting sun.

There was a sadness in his eyes she'd not noticed before.

THE BETTER TO KEEP YOU WITH

I t was bad enough that Judge Redhood was running out
of time, but her employer had given her such a specific
window to work with that the pressure was mounting.
This obsession with time right down to the minute, not to
mention numbers of all kinds, be it currency or characters,
was like a thorn in the judge's side and a royal pain in her ass.
It made her job much more difficult, but she couldn't very
well argue about it. And, she supposed, she was only a
dabbler when it came to magic. She could never cast a spell
of this magnitude, of this duration. So perhaps for an expert
spellmaster those kinds of precise measurements were
important.

The judge herself was not so meticulous. She thought life
should be less rigid and free flowing. It was more interesting
that way. Like when she was married to Robin. She never
knew what her young groom would bring home after a night
of pillaging. Although, now that she thought about it, Robin
rarely let her keep the treasures he found, insisting they go to
the less fortunate. Well, who could be less fortunate than a
wife who didn't have a maid or a sauna?

She frowned as she thought about that last night with him. She had so wanted that locket she found in the mitten.

"But, it's engraved. Surely it's a family heirloom. We can't take a part of someone's history," he had told her "I must return it." Then he left. So she shot him.

She smiled at the thought of his words that night. Because now she had taken all of their histories. And if the curse held, she would have their futures as well.

But she would need to tie up a few loose ends first.

Judge Redhood splashed some cold water on her face in the bathroom and headed back into her secret lair. She checked her phone once more, furious that Tink hadn't shown up or called today. Where was that girl? It had been hours. If Tink had done *her* job properly, the judge would have had more leverage. More bargaining power to present to her cohorts.

She felt the anger bubble in her gut and decided to release it before stepping into the room. She tossed her phone on the ground and stomped it into bitty pieces.

Beside her, Fang howled.

She stroked his fur.

"Shall we?" she asked.

Fang snorted.

Judge Redhood opened the door, preparing herself for round two of battle. She pulled up a scarlet velvet chair and lowered herself into it, taking a few deep breaths to calm her nerves. She stared at the woman across from her.

"Now then. Are you ready to tell me what you've been up to?" the judge asked.

"It's colder than a witch's wart wearing a flannel eye patch in here. Turn the blasted heat on!" Granny said.

The judge pinched the bridge of her nose and closed her eyes. "I should lock you up for butchering the English language."

"I said I'm freezin' me slippers off!"

The judge rose so fast that the chair toppled over behind her, but Granny only scowled.

"Oh you're cold? I'm so sorry. Why don't I make you more comfortable then?" She walked over to the fan standing in the corner of the room, aimed it at the old woman, and switched it on high.

"Now then. I'm only going to ask you this one more time." She inched closer, bent her head to Granny's face. The old woman smelled of menthol and disappointment. "What were you doing at that flea market?"

"I told ya! What's the matter with you? Cat put crayons in your ears?" She rubbed her shoulders, pulled her crocheted sweater tighter around her bosom. "I got a big house with lots of rooms. Can't have them running on empty."

The judge kicked the tufted chair Granny was perched in, but the wrinkled woman just stared at her. "Dammit, you old bat! Are you helping them? Tell me right now," the judge demanded.

Was there a way to reverse the curse somehow? Is that what Granny had been trying to do? And after all the judge had done for her.

Granny said, "I'm hungry. You can't keep a prisoner and not feed it groceries."

"I just fed you." She looked at her watch. "Like an hour ago."

Granny spit on the floor in the vicinity of an untouched dinner tray. "Blech. Tasted like pond scum."

The judge balled up her fists. This was getting her nowhere. She had no idea what Granny had been up to all these weeks, maybe even months. It made her blood boil to think that she had trusted her. That was the last time, she vowed, that she would ever trust a woman. Especially one she was related to.

Fang blew out a sigh behind her and an idea formed in the judge's mind. If Granny wouldn't willingly tell her what she had been doing behind her back, if she wouldn't divulge what she knew about the state of the princesses and their memories, then she'd have to resort to more forceful tactics to extract it.

The judge pivoted and walked to where Fang was lying on a suede sofa. She bent down and whispered in the wolf's ear, keeping a close watch on her grandmother. The old woman squirmed a bit in her seat, but her face was still as stone.

"I have to use the Johnny," Granny said.

Judge Redhood rose, smiled. "Of course." Her voice dripped with venom. "But first, I think I'll leave you alone with Fang for a moment."

Granny sat up straighter in her chair. "You wouldn't do that."

"Try me."

Granny licked her lips and the two women glared at each other for a few moments. Then there was a knock at the door.

Fang, Granny, and Judge Redhood all swung their heads toward the door.

Granny spoke first. "I thought you said no one knows about this room."

"Shh!"

No one did. The room was enchanted as well so that only the judge could open the door to come in or out. She crept toward the door and put her ear to it. There was another knock.

She slowly twisted the knob.

Granny said, "Wait! Don't leave me alone with the wolf."

Judge Redhood looked back. "You had your chance."

"No!" Granny cried and Fang growled.

She slipped out of the room and firmly closed the door behind her.

The ensuing ruckus taking place behind the closed door might have captured the judge's interest under other circumstances, but she was more concerned with what was in front of her.

There, floating on the third floor above a painting of a dark forest, was Tink's shadow.

"What are you doing here? Where is Tink?" asked the judge.

Despite the fact that Tink was also bespelled, her shadow and glitter were still present, although only visible to those who weren't under the influence of the enchantment.

The shadow slumped as if it had a trying day. It couldn't communicate verbally with the judge. It could only make gestures, hear commands and reflect the emotions of its person. From the look of it, it seemed as if Tink was either sleepy or intoxicated.

"That useless little insect. Is she out gallivanting around town when I specifically gave her an assignment?" She crossed her arms.

The shadow tried to shrug, but it bumped into the wall and tumbled to the carpet.

The judge leaned over it. "Stop fooling around. I'll find you a nice jar so you can rest. You'll need it after what I'm going to do to Tink."

The shadow pulled itself up just as the door banged and bulged from within and something in the room crashed into a wall.

For the smallest moment, the judge felt remorse. Then she remembered what Granny had done to her and extinguished it.

She was smiling as she opened the door again, the shadow floating next to her. That smile fell when she saw Granny.

The old woman had a tennis ball in her hand, her arm raised in the air. Fang was across the room, his backside sticking up, tail wagging. He barked. Actually barked like a puppy.

The judge slammed the door. "Are you kidding me?"

Granny tossed Fang the ball and said, "Doctor Bean helped me overcome that fear of wolverines."

Judge Redhood turned and banged her head on the door.

Her secret phone rang. "Now what!"

She unlocked the desk drawer and pulled it out. Lifted it to her ear. "Speak."

Just what she needed. A change in plans.

FOUR BITCHES STEP INTO A CAR

S now sat in the backseat of the car she didn't recognize, wondering what the hell was happening. Punzie seemed to be in a daze. Her braid was curled in her lap, and Bob was perched on her shoulder. She wore a trench coat and sunglasses, and every so often she tapped her bandaged foot. Bob made a *ribbet* sound at Snow, and she nodded at him.

Aura maneuvered the car along the highway, her hand guiding the steering wheel effortlessly. Every once in a while the car gave her directions, and she glanced in her rearview mirror to turn or change lanes. Snow tried to catch her gaze. She wanted to know if Aura had managed to get Bella the book, but that seemed to be low on the priority scale at the moment.

The tension in the vehicle was thick, cut only by Cindy's occasional hiccups.

"Um, Aura, where did you get this car?" Snow finally asked.

"Stole it," Aura said as she took a left turn and coasted the car up a steep hill toward a darkening sky.

Thunder clapped in the distance, threatening a storm.

"You what? Why?" This was so not good. Just because Granny wasn't watching them didn't mean Robin or Tink wasn't. What was going on? Why would she risk getting arrested again when they were so close to the truth?

"You want to take that one, Hot Pants?" Aura said. She turned the car again, then a third time and Snow was certain they were going in circles.

Cindy said, "For fuck's sake, Aura, enough with the roller coaster ride. Are you trying to make me hurl?"

Aura snapped. "I'm trying to make sure we're not being followed. Now lay off the tequila, Cindy, we need all hands on deck. And put those damn shoes on the floor."

Snow peered into the front seat to see Cindy's shoe box perched in her lap. "Why are you carrying your shoes around?" A stolen car and stolen diamond-heeled slippers. Could these women make any more bad decisions?

"No way, Aura. I know you've got your greedy eye on them. I'm not letting these babies out of my sight. You'll need to pry them from my cold, dead hands."

"That can be arranged," Aura said as she made yet another turn and headed up toward the canyon.

"Will someone please tell me what's going on?" Snow asked.

Cindy craned her neck around to look at Snow. "Sure. Cupcake over here killed a guy." She thumbed to Punzie

Snow snapped her head to Punzie who finally seemed to wake up. She kicked the back of Cindy's seat. Cindy made an "oof" sound and spilled some tequila.

"Shut up, Cindy. You were there, you saw. He attacked me."

"How?" Snow asked.

"That's your question? How?" Aura said.

Snow's head was reeling. A moment ago, she was frantic

because she was sitting in a stolen car with stolen merchandise thinking they'd all be facing court charges again. Now she feared they would never be free of Everafter.

"What happened, Punzie?" Snow asked.

Punzie said, "I don't want to talk about it. Let's just get this over with and never speak of it again."

Cindy scoffed. "Oh sure, that'll be easy as pie." She tried to snap her fingers, but they weren't cooperating.

"Aura, I demand to know where we're going," Snow said.

Punzie and Cindy both looked at Snow as if she had just dug her own grave. Aura raised one brow and caught Snow's eye in the rearview mirror.

Snow was getting tired of playing meek, but she supposed now wasn't the time to split hairs. "Please."

Aura sighed. "Apparently some guy came in as Punzie was wrapping up her set."

"To the jukebox. Goddamn DJ was in the back boinking the next act."

Aura rolled her eyes. "To the jukebox. Punzie was on stage, he grabbed her from behind and she head-butted him. He flew across the stage and smacked his head on a speaker."

"And it was lights out," Cindy said.

"But it was an accident," said Snow. "You didn't mean to hurt him. And you were defending yourself."

"I *did* mean to hurt him. Didn't mean to kill him," Punzie said. "And do you really think the judge would believe me? My only witness is a boozy blonde divorcée with a chip on her shoulder and a history of violence against men."

Cindy said, "Girl power!"

Punzie shook her head and looked out the window at the passing mountains. "Redhood wouldn't buy it. That woman would lock up her own grandmother if she had the chance."

Snow snapped to attention. She looked at Punzie. "What did you say?"

"I said she'd never believe me."

"No, the other thing."

Bob hopped into Punzie's lap and she tickled his nose. He cooed. "Oh, that she'd lock up her own grandmother? Wouldn't put it past her."

Snow met Aura's eyes in the mirror. Could Granny be Red Riding Hood's grandmother? If that was the case, did she know it here in this land? And would she come looking for her?

Then another thought hit Snow. "This man, was he the same man as before?" Snow asked. The writer couldn't die. He couldn't. Because where would that leave them? They might never find any answers.

"No, I don't think so. This guy had a beard and long hair. The other guy was bald."

Snow felt the slightest relief, but she was still mortified that now they were all accomplices to a man's demise. And that someone had tried to hurt Punzie. Did it have anything to do with what was happening to them?

"And Cindy? Why were you there?" Snow asked.

Cindy buffed her nails. "I had nothing better to do, so I was there for the free booze. I was the only one, though. You must not be a hot ticket anymore with that bum foot."

Punzie sneered at Cindy's back. "First of all, I could wear a garbage bag and I would still be the hottest ticket in town thanks to Destiny and Star."

"Who?" said Snow.

Aura said, "She's talking about her boobs."

Punzie said, "Second, the drinks are not free, moron. You have a tab as long as my braid," Punzie said.

Cindy frowned. "Really?"

"Can we get back on track?" Snow said.

Aura sighed. "Cindy helped wrapped the guy up in a rug, and then tweedle dumb and tweedle dumber over here called me to get rid of the evidence." Cindy punched Aura in the arm as she took another turn. Aura slugged her back. "I certainly wasn't going to load a stiff into my own car, so I borrowed this one and we hauled him into the trunk."

Snow felt like she was going to be sick. She squirmed at the thought of a dead man in the trunk of the car just behind her. She couldn't wrap her brain around it. Couldn't believe things had gone this far. Punzie was a princess. A queen actually, but none of them liked to use the term now that they'd united the kingdoms of Enchantment. She was a noble woman, a woman of substance and power, compassion and vigor. Now she had blood on her hands. It made Snow's heart heavy.

"So why did you pick me up?" Snow asked, but she knew the answer the moment Aura shot her a look through the rearview mirror. Aura was probably going to insist Cindy touch the shoes, and she wanted Snow there when Cindy's memory came back. They were all in this together. Especially now. Punzie's crime was their shared crime.

Cindy said, "In for a penny..." She looked out the window as she tried to recall the rest of that phrase. "Or something. I don't know, I've never actually seen a penny." She burped.

Punzie said, "Why is this taking so long? We should have been there by now."

"Because, Mistress Manslaughter, I'm making sure we're not being followed."

Punzie stuck her tongue out at Aura's back.

Cindy said, "I called Bella too. She knows. She's supposed to meet us there."

Snow and Aura locked eyes. *She knows?* The blank look on Aura's face didn't give Snow any hints as to what had transpired between her and Bella.

So was she back? Did she remember? More importantly, what were they going to do now?

RED, RED, ROSE

Being magically delinquent sucks. For one thing, you can't bespell anyone to do your dirty work like slap the newspaper boy when he tosses the daily into the bushes, throw coffee into a barista's face when she gets the order wrong, or kill Snow White. Judge Redhood paced the room, chewing on a fingernail, and tried to come up with a good candidate for a murder for hire plot.

Giant Jerry might do it, but he'd be too conspicuous. Most people ran screaming in the other direction whenever they saw him walking down the street. Tink could probably be persuaded to do the job, loyal little sprite that she was, but the judge still had not heard word one from that girl. Her shadow was resting comfortably in a jar on the side table beneath a lamp. You would think she would have sensed it missing and come looking for it. Though perhaps not, since she wasn't a complete version of her true self in this land. While the curse erased the memories of Enchantment, replacing them with memories of growing up in Everafter, people still retained the core of their being. Their nature, if you will. Which was why Robin Hood still believed in helping people and doing the 'right' thing. It was annoying.

The judge certainly couldn't kill Snow White herself. Not that she was opposed to murder, per say, but the manner in which the execution was to take place—or more accurately, the proof her conspirators insisted on—was far too gory for her tastes. The judge wasn't fond of blood—if it was up to her, she'd just feed the privileged princess a poisoned apple. Sometimes the oldest ideas were the best ones. No muss, no fuss. But her orders were to deliver Snow White's heart on a silver platter.

Royals. They were so dramatic.

The judge could feel Fang's eyes on her as she took another lap around the room.

"Don't do this," Granny said. "You'll regret it. It'll squeal at you for the rest of your life."

"Shut up, Grandmother. It's your fault we're in this mess. I had no intention of killing any of them. I just wanted them to suffer as I had. But I've been backed into a corner now, thanks to you."

"You still have choices. There's still time."

Time. That word again. Although time had been on her side in Everafter. It was slower here somehow. An entire year had already passed in Enchantment. Had she known that when she signed up for this gig, she would have paid closer attention to the date. She had only just realized that tonight was the deadline for the curse to expire should the princesses find a way to break it. If they didn't, they would be trapped in Everafter forever, living out their days as wayward women. But they were together now, which meant the magic could find them, and would, thanks to Granny's meddling. It took some doing, but the judge had finally wrenched the truth out of the old woman. It was amazing how fast you could get someone to talk when you held their hand over a hot flame.

Granny, it turned out, had been stockpiling objects that represented the storybook worlds. All the worlds, in fact. Worlds that had nothing to do with Enchantment, and of course the ones that did. Her hope had been to find the one object that held magic strong enough to break the spell. It was ingenious really. But the judge wasn't very worried about that. She had made certain that the place was void of magic, save for the little she had brought herself. And the largest threat—mirrors—she had eliminated upon arrival.

That didn't mean that some magic hadn't slipped through the veil. After all, Tink's shadow shouldn't have passed through at all, yet it had been there from the beginning, unbeknownst to the fairy. So there was the tiniest possibility that residual magic had attached itself to others as well.

Which meant the princesses could find it. And the judge suspected they were working on that very thing as she paced.

Why did Snow White have to set that fire! Animals don't need justice. She and her highfalutin' morals. They ruined everything.

Granny said, "It could backfire right in your eye socket, you know. Whatever puppet put you up to this could open its maw and eat you right up."

The judge looked at her and smiled. "I don't think so. You see, I'm not a princess, am I Granny?"

Granny winced as if she'd been slapped. "Quit festering on them open sores."

"I think you mean don't open old wounds."

"What have you."

"Well, you were right the first time. That wound is still open. But I intend to close it. I just need to figure out how."

The judge did another lap and stopped in front of Tink's

shadow, sleeping so peacefully. She tapped the glass and the shadow stirred. An idea was forming.

"Why her? Why Snow White?" Granny asked in a solemn voice.

"Because she's the queen. Everyone knows that when you take over a kingdom, you have to kill the queen."

The judge didn't think it possible, but Granny's face took on more wrinkles. "They all be princesses. It's in the treaty."

The judge scoffed. "Oh please. Just because they insist they run a kind of democracy doesn't make it true. There can only be one ruler, and that ruler is Snow White. The first princess."

A bee flew in through the open window and the judge watched it fly around the room. She rarely opened the window in this room, but setting someone's hand on fire gives off a noxious odor.

The bee landed on the desk and the judge watched it a minute longer. What happened to the rest of the colony when its queen bee died, she wondered? Did it appoint another? Or did one simply take over?

The bee flew towards her, and the judge reached out and grabbed it. She smashed it in her hand. Then she called Fang to her and unhooked his collar. She unzipped a pocket inside it and pulled out a tiny purple pill. She walked over to the table and picked up Tink's shadow. Unscrewed the jar.

"No, don't do it, Missy!"

The judge ignored Granny as she plopped the tablet inside the jar with the sleeping shadow. She twisted the lid back in place, held the jar with both hands and closed her eyes, softly chanting the instructions that would send her servant on its deadly errand.

She opened her eyes and watched as the shadow awoke, yawned and stood.

Then she walked over to the open window.

Granny shouted, "Snow White is still your sister! You can't do this!"

The judge slowly turned and said, "She hasn't been my sister for a long time. You made sure of that, didn't you, Granny?"

Granny shook her head. "I did my best, Rose Red. I swear on a dictionary, I did."

She shot the old woman an icy stare. "Don't ever call me that again. My name is Red Riding Hood."

She opened the jar and the shadow flew out the window.

"No! You can't un-ring that pot!" Granny cried.

Red Riding Hood looked at her grandmother. "Too late. Snow White dies tonight."

Then, with the bit of magic left on her fingertips, she waved her hand toward Granny's mouth, gluing the old woman's lips shut.

"I never could stand the way you talked, Granny."

MEANWHILE, BACK AT THE RANCH

R obin Hood clutched the papers in his hand and slowly turned around. "Easy there, boy."

The dog's head hung low to the ground and his hackles were on point. Robin almost always had something to munch on in one of his pockets or beneath his hat, but a quick search found no food source that he could bribe the dog with. He stuffed the papers into an inside pocket.

Beast let out a growl that sounded more like a bear than a canine. Robin backed up as Beast circled over to him, his fierce eyes locked onto Robin's. He wasn't that far from the front door. If he could only inch backward, he'd be close enough to make a run for it.

As if sensing Robin's plan, Beast changed direction, herding Robin away from the door. A few more stealth maneuvers on the dog's part, and Robin found himself facing the parlor.

"Come on, Beast. You know me. You see me every week, buddy."

Beast roared, and Robin nearly soiled his pants.

Of all the grief and turmoil this house and its inhabitants

had brought him, none of them had injected this level of fear. He found himself re-thinking his entire career path. Perhaps thieving really *was* his calling. He hadn't ever broken into a home or a business with a dog the size of a dump truck inside. He was careful back then—cautious. Every job was mapped out ahead of time, and if there was so much as a floodlight, he would pass on the opportunity. Marion would understand if he went back to that life. Perhaps he could even partner up with Aura.

Beast grumbled, and Robin wondered if it was possible Bella had trained the dog to attack him specifically? Of course it was. Robin eyed his surroundings as Beast stood there, drool pouring from his sharp fangs and pooling around his lion-sized paws. One of the doors beyond the parlor led to that bizarre clock room. The other, Robin hadn't checked out. What if it was locked?

He looked at Beast. The dog gave him a savage stare. He tried to calculate the time it would take him to reach the door and how long it would take the dog to reach his backside.

Six of one, he thought. He cracked his knuckles. Should he attempt it?

Robin hadn't yet made his decision when Beast advanced on him, jaws snapping. Robin ran faster than he had in his entire life, not caring that he was screaming in a most undig-nified pitch. He wrenched the closet door open, flew inside, and slammed it shut behind him just as Beast jumped up, batting his giant paws at the heavy wood. The dog barked as Robin fumbled for a light switch. He finally found one and clicked the light on.

Beast's howls subsided and Robin put his ear to the keyhole. He heard the dog grunt, take a deep breath, then flop onto the floor just outside the door. He snorted, grum-bled, and let out a sigh like a diesel engine braking.

Robin was trapped. Terrific, he thought. Marion would be worried sick.

He turned around to assess his new temporary home. The room was the size of a small office or a nursery, and painted a pale blue. Piles upon piles of Granny's treasures were neatly stacked against the walls, as if someone had been in here recently taking inventory. It was clean too, not nearly as dusty as the closet he had explored earlier or the room with the numbers and timepieces. He spotted a spinning wheel, stacks of books, various tea sets, boxes of shoes, a scarecrow, and in one corner, a mountain of playing cards. He knew that Granny used to play bingo often. Perhaps the cards were prizes she'd won.

Robin stepped over a picnic basket and grabbed a deck with a picture of a forest on the box. He may as well play solitaire, since he would likely be stuck here for a while. At least until one of the girls or Granny came home. He dragged a folding table and chairs from against the back wall, plopped the cards down, removed his hat, and sat.

He took the crumpled papers from inside his jacket and started reading. He found himself looking at a property abstract for Granny's house. It contained a survey of the land, the address, tax identification number, and the deed. He flipped through the pages, expecting to find a list of owners over the years, as all abstracts contained, but oddly enough, only one was listed.

Judge Redhood.

Robin scratched his head. That couldn't be right. He flipped through the pages again and again and not only were there no previous owners listed, but Granny's name was nowhere to be found.

Robin sat back in the chair and set the papers on the table. He stood up and walked the space, examining the chipped woodwork, the faded carpet peeling up from the hardwood floors, the antique brass doorknob etched with roses.

He tapped an old typewriter that was anchoring a leaning stack of books. There was a thought, an idea, maybe even a memory knocking at the back of his brain, but he couldn't reach it. It might be feasible that Granny had fallen behind on the mortgage and perhaps the town had taken over the home for use as government housing. But then why would it be in the judge's name?

More disturbingly, it made no sense that a home well over a hundred years old had no previous owner except a judge who was barely thirty. What was going on? And what was that bitch up to?

Robin sat back down and sifted through the papers, looking for more clues as to what was happening in Everafter and specifically, this house. He read them backwards and forwards. He flipped them over and laid them back on the table. It was then he noticed something printed on the back of the deed in letters so small that he couldn't make them out.

He had nothing but time. He searched through the piles of antiques, collectibles, and utterly useless junk until he uncovered an old medical bag with a magnifying glass tucked inside. He grabbed it and sat back down to examine the fine print.

It read, "In lieu of deed, exemption is granted to Granny from the curse."

Robin sat back and scratched his head.

What the heck did that mean? *Curse?* He was beginning to wonder if anything—or *anyone*—in this town was what they seemed.

Something rustled in the left corner of the room, and he thought he saw movement. A trick of the light? He went to investigate anyway and discovered a brown mouse perched atop a quiver of arrows next to the most beautiful bow he had ever seen. It was hand crafted—a work of art, actually—etched with leaves and vines, and hand-painted in shades of green, maple, and coffee.

He picked it up.

SOMETHING BITCHY THIS WAY
COMES

A t the top of Forest Canyon Lane, beneath an ever-darkening sky pierced by streaks of angry indigo, a cricket chirped. It was the only sound that interrupted the thoughts of four princesses who stared into the trunk of a stolen car at a very alive man. His eyes were huge pools of blue as he blinked up at them. There was the slightest trickle of blood near his left temple, and the rug he was wrapped in smelled of beer, cigarettes, and shame.

The women were stunned into stilled silence for a several moments. All except Bella who was about to lean into the trunk, an enormous knife in her hand.

Snow grabbed her arm and said, "No!"

Bella looked at Snow, winked, and said, "Relax, Princess."

The tone she used as she said those words, the gleam in her eyes. "Bella?" Snow asked.

Aura grinned. Punzie and Cindy shared a confused look.

Bella smiled coyly, then bent over the man and cut the ropes that bound him. She placed the knife in Snow's hand and got to work unraveling Punzie's victim from the filthy rug.

A stout, middle-aged man with a face like a basset hound accepted Bella's assistance and climbed out of the trunk.

He stood there, looking from one to the other of them, shirt rumpled, pants soiled with dirt and grime from the floor of the strip club. He removed a wig and fake beard, tossing them onto the dusty road.

"Grimm!" Snow cried and hugged him.

He stiffened under her grip at first, then relaxed and patted her back. "Yes, yes. I've missed you too."

Punzie wrenched the knife from Snow's grip and held it up to the writer's neck. "Who are you? What do you want with me?"

Grimm rolled his eyes and said, "You always were the stubborn one, Punzie. I take it you didn't receive my note."

Snow stepped forward and said, "Punzie, release that blade at once!"

Punzie sneered at Snow. "Who the fuck do you think you are? This lunatic tried to attack me, remember? Twice!"

Grimm rolled his eyes. "Such language in this land. I would have written you better than that."

Punzie's face distorted into a mix of curiosity and bafflement. "What the hell does that mean?"

Bella yanked the knife from Punzie's arm and lobbed it into the canyon.

Punzie said, "What is *wrong* with you two?" She glared at Bella and Snow.

Grimm rubbed his bald head and said, "I see we are not all on the same page."

"I'm afraid not," Snow said.

Aura said, "I think we can change that." She jogged to the passenger side of the car and grabbed Cindy's shoes.

"Damn it, Aura, you can't have them!" Cindy barked. Then she hiccupped and unscrewed her flask.

"May I?" Grimm held his palm out.

Cindy shrugged. "Knock yourself out." She offered him the liquor.

Grimm grabbed the flask and threw it into the canyon after the knife.

Cindy watched, dumbfounded, as the tequila sailed out of sight. She pivoted to Grimm. "You son of a bitch!"

She lunged at the scribe and in that moment, Aura held a shoe up. "Ah, ah, ah. No killing anyone or the crystal slipper gets it." Aura held the heel with one hand and the toe with the other.

Cindy's face drained of color. Then her eyes darkened to the shade of the stormy clouds. She dropped her hands to her hips. "You wouldn't dare."

Aura said, "Wanna bet?"

The two women stared at each other for a beat. Then Cindy made a mad dash for the shoe and grabbed it in both hands. She stopped short. As if she'd hit a wall.

Snow, Bella, Aura, and Grimm studied Cindy's face for a hint of recognition. She stared at the shoe with an intensity Snow had not seen since they'd met in Everafter. The honey-haired princess peered into the prism of the diamond heel, holding it up to the sun. Her eyes brightened to their original cerulean blue and she blinked several times, twisting her neck like a curious sparrow peeking through a window. Her features softened, her face filled with wonder.

Then she screamed and dropped the crystal shoe. They all watched as it shattered against a boulder, the diamond burning up under a slim ray of the last light of day. Then it melted into the road and was gone.

Cindy turned to Snow and said, "What happened? What are we doing here?"

Grimm smiled. "Four down, one to go."

They all turned to Punzie, who wrapped her braid around her wrist and backed up nervously, Bob at her side. "I don't know what you wackos are up to, but stay the fuck away from me."

"Punzie…" Snow said.

Punzie turned and began teetering down the unpaved road in her stilettos. She waved a hand behind her head. "Nope. Punzie has left the building. So long, psychos."

"She never was the *brightest* princess," Grimm said.

"Bite me, weirdo," Punzie called and made an obscene gesture.

Snow said, "Where's her nemesis, Grimm? Do you know? I haven't seen a tower anywhere in Everafter."

Grimm said, "Well of course not, it would have been a bit conspicuous, a big tower like that just appearing overnight."

"Unlike, say, an apple tree," Bella smirked.

Grimm gave a sheepish look. "Yes well, I forgot that when it comes to the first princess, subtle magic is best. It was supposed to be just one apple, but Snow's strength made it explode into that monstrosity."

Snow watched Punzie stumble along the path, Bob hopping happily beside her. One of her heels broke and she faltered, then removed both shoes and chucked them into the canyon.

Cindy said, "That canyon's eating a lot of litter today."

Bella said, "I'll get her."

Snow watched as Bella jogged down the path. She turned to Grimm. "So it was you who sent our story enemies?"

Grimm said, "Aye. When you signed the blood treaty, do you remember the clause that said it couldn't be broken without all of your consent?"

The three princesses nodded.

Grimm said, "Yes, well I added the most miniscule fine print to the treaty that should any of you turn on one another, or fall prey to a curse, your story nemeses would act as talismans. They are bound to each of you, but they need magic to find you. That's why it's taken so long. There is no magic in this land, so I had to get a bit—shall we say —creative."

Bella was arguing with Punzie on the road. Punzie tried to kick her and Bella grabbed her foot. They both tumbled to the dirt.

Aura said, "What do you mean, creative?"

"I mean I wrote. Short stories, mostly. Hoping that my words would find you or at the very least, that they would bring me visions of your whereabouts."

Cindy said, "So *you* did all of this?"

Grimm cringed. "Heavens no! I could never create such a garish place." He looked at the silver car as if it were an alien from another planet. "No, I wrote happy tales of the five of you living prosperously."

Aura said, "Well, I hate to break it to you, Grimm, but this isn't exactly Paradise on a platter."

Grimm sighed. "Alas readers don't enjoy stories without conflict, and without readers, the written word has no meaning. No life force. The words weren't finding you, so I had to make them darker."

"So you wrote me as a *car thief?*" Aura asked.

Grimm snorted. "Of course not! Never even seen vehicles such as they own in this land." He looked across the canyon, down to the town below where the lights were popping on one by one. Rock music drifted up to the peak. Far off, a car horn blared. "Such a noisy, place too."

Grimm brought his focus back to the ladies. "I wrote tales of sinister witches and smelly trolls. I had no idea you had all succumbed to *this.*" He swept his hand across the canyon and below. "There is something though," he added.

"What is it?" Snow asked.

"I was given orders. Orders to change the endings of your

biographies." He explained how he was to insert the word *in* before ever after.

Snow said, "Orders from whom?"

"I don't know. It was a royal order, written on a palace scroll and sealed with a royal seal. At first I thought the five of you had wanted the change. I thought perhaps after the kingdoms united, after the wars, you may have wanted a fresh start by changing the name of the land."

Snow asked, "Who signed the order?"

Grimm gave Snow a stoic look. "You did, your Majesty."

Cindy and Aura snapped their heads to Snow.

"No, that's not true. Someone falsified my signature." Snow looked at her blood-oath sisters. "I swear it on my heart."

Grimm bowed his head. "I realize that now. Especially after all that's happened in Enchantment."

"What's happened, Grimm? What has become of our kingdom?"

Grimm looked up and said, "First, I need all of you. There's not much time left, and I fear I may be pulled back soon. I have only so much magic to keep me anchored to this land." Grimm shifted his gaze to the one princess who had yet to recover her memory.

Bella was dragging Punzie up the road by her braid. Punzie protested the entire way, kicking, screaming, and swearing. At one point, she bit Bella, who cried out in pain and bitch-slapped Punzie.

Aura asked, "What is Punzie's talisman if not the tower?"

"If she had read the note I tried to slip her the first time she attacked me she would have known." Grimm grimaced at the memory. "My neck still hurts. Of course I lied and gave the name Story to the police officer." He looked from one of them to the other. "There's no telling who is friend and who is foe."

Bella had Punzie's braid wrapped around her wrist in a tight grip as they joined the others.

"What did the note say, Grimm?" Bella asked, breathless, while Punzie tried to shake loose.

Punzie spat, "I'm calling Doc when we get back to the house. He's going to throw all of you in the looney bin."

Grimm rolled his eyes at Punzie, turned to Bella and said, "As I told your blood-oath sisters, I had to get creative. For example, I sent Aura the wheel via her fairy godmother."

Fear shadowed Aura's face for a moment and thunder rumbled in the sky.

Grimm looked at the clouds, concerned. "Don't worry, your Majesty, it was the good one."

Aura blew out a sigh of relief.

Punzie said, "Your majesty? Did I fall down a wormhole? Did I get into Cindy's tequila or eat some magic mushrooms or something?"

"Grimm, the note," said Snow.

"Right so. It read simply, 'Kiss the Frog.'"

Twelve pairs of eyes fastened on Bob, who perked up and stood taller. He looked at Punzie with woeful admiration.

Punzie looked at Bob and said, "Now I know you're all bonkers."

Bob deflated.

Cindy said, "Damn it, Punzie just kiss the frog and this will all make sense."

Punzie said, "You know, Cindy, I wish you could hear yourself sometimes. In what world does kissing a frog make sense?"

"In our world," said Snow. "Kiss the frog."

Punzie crossed her arms.

Aura said, "Come on Tassel Tosser. Kiss the frog."

"You could do worse. And I'm pretty sure you have," Bella said. "Kiss the damn frog."

"No!" shouted Punzie.

Grimm, Snow, Aura, Bella, and Cindy all yelled, "Kiss the frog!"

"Oh for fuck's sake, fine!"

Punzie bent down and kissed Bob on the tip of his bulbous nose.

In a haze of purple smoke, Bob puffed and jutted and grew to a height of six feet. His green skin faded to a fleshy tan, human looking arms grew from his torso, and his sinewy legs bulged into muscular limbs. The smoke thickened and for a moment he was gone and then, after the cloud cleared, prince Ashford appeared.

Punzie sucked in her breath, not taking her eyes off her love. She rushed forward to embrace her prince. "Ashford!" She cried.

Ashford caught her in his arms and kissed her. Then, like a whisper, he faded away.

Punzie spun around. "Where did he go?"

Grimm gave her a sad look. "I'm afraid I was only able to capture him for a moment, your Majesty. He has returned to Enchantment."

Snow stepped forward and embraced Punzie. A single tear slid down her porcelain cheek and she asked Snow, "What's happened to us?"

"That, my blood-sister, is what I intend to find out," Snow said.

Snow turned to see Bella staring at where Ashford had stood only moments ago, a frown on her face.

"What is it, Bella?" she asked.

"I'm just wondering." She cocked her head toward Grimm. "Is Beast...the dog, I mean...is that *my* Beast?"

"That enormous canine? No, no." Grimm shook his head vehemently.

Bella sighed in relief. "Thank God. The things I've seen that dog do to himself..."

"There isn't much time," Grim said. "With the first drop of rain, I'll be gone. So I want you to listen and listen good. There is talk of a curse. After you disappeared, the kingdom was left in chaos. No one has stepped in to lead, and Enchantment has fallen into a state of mayhem. Many have fled the kingdom entirely. I fear the curse was cast as a plot to take over the land."

"Have you any idea who's behind the curse?" Snow asked.

"Nay, but it must be someone of great power. I haven't seen magic of this magnitude in Enchantment since before the treaty."

Cindy said, "An evil queen?"

Aura said, "A witch?"

Grimm shook his head, "I truly don't know, but whoever it is is strong. Stronger than you can imagine. And I suspect they may be stealing magic, as it's difficult to come by these days."

Snow considered Grimm's words. "There's a room in Granny's house. Filled with clocks and watches and numbers. It reminds me of no story I have ever read."

Grimm thought for a moment. "Nor I. It isn't mine, and it isn't my brother's. But it may mean something else."

"What?" Aura asked.

Grimm hesitated, but Bella tapped him on the shoulder. "Spill," she said.

"It has been nearly a year since you and many others vanished from Enchantment."

The women gasped and began firing off questions one by one.

The clouds rolled in faster now and thunder boomed directly over their heads.

Grimm looked up with worry. He stretched his arms out.

"There's no time for questions, nor have I answers, so gather round, princesses."

The five women huddled around the scribe. "Each of you is like a daughter to me and each of you has seen her fair share of strife. As individual women, you are strong, fierce, and powerful. As a unit, you must also be loyal, honest, and brave. You've been all those things in the past and you can be again. You must trust each other, rely on each other. Always remember that together, you can accomplish anything. For it was the five of you who brought peace to Enchantment."

They nodded.

"Now, go get your kingdom back."

A drop of rain splattered on Grimm's shoe.

And he was gone.

A WOLF IN SHEEP'S CLOTHING

The five princesses left the stolen vehicle at the top of the canyon and piled into Bella's car. There were more pressing matters to attend to. Like where was Granny? Who was behind the curse? And who, in this land, was friend and who was foe?

Snow racked her brain to come up with a logical enemy. They all had villains, to be sure, but most of those axes had been ground out years ago.

The answers, she was certain, were back at Granny's house.

Granny's house. Funny how magic began to find Snow as soon as she stepped inside that place. Odd too, that none of the others felt it before she arrived. And that she was the first to recover her memory.

But, as Grimm said, she was the first princess.

Unless...was this all because of her? Was the curse somehow linked to Snow? Was it really a coup? Or did someone hate her so much that they would go to such extreme lengths to dispose of her? She could recall no enemy so grave, but if that was the case, then it was because of her that Enchantment and its people were left without their leaders.

The storm blew into town with them, the rain pelting the windshield like pebbles. Bella turned the wipers to high. She briefly explained that she had managed to get Tink into the school and that last she saw, the sprite was being hauled off to the detention quarters by an angry teacher.

Punzie sat next to Snow her braid curled around her waist. Every so often she asked a question and Snow and Aura tried to fill in the gaps of her awareness with what they knew—and what they didn't. Every so often, she reached in her pocket as if Bob was still nestled there.

Bella said, "I want to examine those rooms, Snow. The minute we get back."

Snow agreed. The ballroom, the room with the clocks, the locked room that not even Aura had a key to open. What did it contain?

They drove the rest of the way to the house in silence, with only the drum of rain accompanying their thoughts. They had a mission now—one that was even more daunting than the ogre problem they had faced all those years ago.

An entire year. They had been away from the kingdom, their people, for an entire year.

All that they had worked for, all that they had built, gone in a flash.

Her anger built as the car crested the hill to the darkened, dilapidated home. *Oh yes, someone will pay for this.*

The women got out of the car and entered the house.

There was no sign of Granny. No lights on, no smells of coffee or food, no footsteps, no piles of "treasures." Just the eager panting of Beast, who greeted them excitedly.

Bella ushered the dog into the kitchen while Aura ran upstairs to collect the key ring she had copied from Granny's master set. Punzie volunteered to get Granny's inventory notebook, and Cindy ran to retrieve the notes Snow had taken on her exploration. They moved like a well-orchestrated symphony, each doing her part. Like the old days.

Snow wound her way around the house to the locked room. She turned the handle, knowing it wouldn't open, but she had to try. She had to do something.

She heard Bella call to her. "Snow, come on. Show me that room you were telling Grimm about. He might not know the story, but I may."

Snow ran back through the parlor and met up with Aura, Punzie, Cindy, and Bella.

"I've got the key here somewhere," Aura said, shuffling through the huge ring.

Punzie flipped through the notebook, searching for a clue, as Aura slipped a key into the lock. The door creaked open, and Snow and Bella stepped inside the cramped space that held nothing but numbers and timepieces.

"I can't make heads or tails of it," Snow said.

Bella approached the lower shelf first. She tentatively touched each clock and watch that she could reach. She closed her eyes, concentrating.

Snow watched as Bella moved her hands along the next shelf and the next, picking up ticking timepieces one by one.

She stopped abruptly, examining an alarm clock with closer scrutiny. It was set to six o'clock. Bella picked it up, turned it over in her hands. Snow studied her and by the twitch of her cheek, knew there was an idea forming in Bella's mind. She set it back down, then picked up another clock shaped like a cat. Its eyes bulged and its tail swayed. Snow thought it was the ugliest thing she had ever seen.

Bella took a step back, looking at the numbers on the walls. Some were multiplication problems that didn't add up—4x5=12, 4x6=13. Some were random numbers—2, 5, 7. She inched forward again, picked up another clock in the shape of a white rabbit with pink eyes and a bell between its ears. She stepped back again. She touched a heart-shaped watch, then snapped her hand away as if she'd been burned.

Her face twisted with rage. She turned to look at the other princesses. "I can't believe it."

"What? What is it?" Snow asked.

"Do you know who's behind this?" asked Aura.

Cindy said, "Is it my stepmother?"

Punzie was still flipping through the book. "There's nothing in here. No names anyway."

"Don't any of you read?" Bella snapped.

Cindy looked at Punzie. "I like romance novels."

Punzie shrugged. "Do bathroom walls count?"

"I'm a mystery fan," said Snow.

"Me too," said Aura. "Hey, have you read—"

"Shut up!" Bella ran a hand through her dark waves. "Look closer at the clocks. The heart, the cat, the white rabbit." She stepped forward and pulled out a clock in the shape of a deck of cards. "Playing cards. Ring a bell?"

Snow looked at each item. The clocks ticked away and chimed, mocking the thoughts running through her head.

She gasped, met Bella's stare. "No, it can't be."

"Oh but it is, my pale friend," Bella said.

"Alice?" Snow looked at her compatriots.

"That bitch!" said Punzie. "After we granted her asylum from Wanderland?"

"But she's only a kid," said Cindy. "Barely twenty."

Aura said, "A kid who once ruled her own kingdom, don't forget." Aura sighed, looked at the others. "So now what?"

Snow said, "Now we find a way home. And we start by breaking into that locked room. Maybe there's a mirror in there. Maybe more than one."

"Would a mirror be enough to make magic?" Cindy asked.

"Perhaps. With the apples," Snow said, "Only one way to find out."

Aura said, "I told you, Snow, that thing is a fortress. No one's getting in there. There's not a key that works and nothing in my arsenal can penetrate that lock."

Snow smiled. "Then we break it down."

THE RAIN POURED down on her in buckets as Snow jogged out to the shed to retrieve the ax. She stepped over the bag of apples, around a lawn mower, a hedge trimmer, and seven shovels, but she couldn't find the ax anywhere. She had just seen it when she grabbed the chainsaw to cut the tree down not more than a day ago. Where was it?

"You looking for this?"

Snow spun to face Hansel. He was sopping wet, muddy, and haggard. His tee shirt clung to him, his jeans were soaked through. He looked like something that had crawled out of a grave. The ax rested casually on his shoulder, and Snow was about to say yes, but something in his tone and his stance stopped her. A flash of lightning lit his features and revealed Tink's black shadow hovering over him. Attached to him.

Snow backed up slowly. She felt behind her for one of the shovels. "Hansel, what are you doing?"

She found a handle, gripped it.

"The queen of hearts must have her parts," Hansel said mechanically.

"Is that what Alice is calling herself these days?" Snow asked.

She tightened her grip on the shovel.

Hansel hefted the ax in his hand. "The queen of hearts must have her parts."

He sprang on her then, so fast that she didn't have time to

bring the shovel around. Instead, she spun away from him and the ax bit into the shed wall. He pulled at it, grunting.

Snow grabbed the shovel and swung it at Hansel's head. The blow connected, but it only dazed him. He yanked the ax out of the wall with a roar, pivoted, and crouched into a fighting stance.

Snow matched his movements. She planted her feet, ready for the next attack. "Hansel, do not do this. This isn't you."

Hansel let out a warrior cry and lunged at her. Snow fended off the ax with her shovel. The shock of the blow hurt her hands. The clang of metal crashing into metal echoed through the small shed, stinging her eardrums, overpowered only by the booming thunder.

If she could just hold on, just maneuver until her back was to the shed door, she could flee.

And then what?

Hansel said, robotically, "I must have your heart. It's in the cards." He swung the ax at her head, but she ducked under the blow.

"Over my dead body!" She used the shovel to push him, and he stumbled back, tripping over a hose.

Snow saw her opportunity and dashed around Hansel, but he grabbed her ankle and she smacked to the floor. She grabbed the shovel and struck his hand where it gripped her leg. He cried out and let go.

Snow scrambled to her feet and ran, but stumbled over the sack of apples and flew out of the shed. She slid into mud, cold grass and slimy leaves. The apple sack was just within reach. She stuck her arm inside it, felt around.

Rotten. All of them. She flipped over, but before she could stand, Hansel was straddling her.

He lifted the ax high above his head and she shielded herself with the blade of the shovel. The ax came down with a *whoosh* as Snow cried out. The blade cracked in two, the pieces spiraling to either side. One struck Hansel's left arm, spearing through his bicep and knocking him away.

Snow flipped onto her stomach and crawled a few pitiful inches before Hansel grabbed her feet and yanked her back. She squirmed out of his grip and rolled over searching for something to hit him with. There was nothing but the apples. Hansel still had one good arm and the only weapon. She couldn't outrun him. She was no match for his strength.

She wasn't going to survive this.

Her last thought, before she put the mushy apple pulp to her lips was—*This is all my fault. It's me they're after.* Perhaps if she was gone, the spell would be broken and the other princesses—and Enchantment itself—could be saved.

And so she bit into the sour apple meat, knowing that it was the less painful way to die.

An arrow buzzed over her head, piercing Hansel's neck and Tink's shadow all at once. Hansel's eyes widened in shock. The ax slipped from his hands and fell to his side. His body collapsed next to Snow's.

Snow looked up. "Robin Hood."

He bowed. "At your service, your Majesty."

Snow scrambled to her feet and picked up the ax. Something had been niggling at her mind, something about Alice's story. Something about time and a year…and the whole world crashed into her at once. *We've already been here close to a year,* Grimm had said. *There's almost no time left.* And Snow was not about to allow her people to remain trapped in Everafter. Not as long as there was life left in her.

"Robin, thank you. I have to—"

"Go!" he said.

Even as her strength ebbed, Snow rushed back into the house, back to that locked room, and called for the others in a weakened voice.

Footsteps rang behind her as she reached that forbidden room. Footsteps that seemed miles away.

She lifted the ax with both hands, and with the last drop of her strength, shattered the thick door with one blow.

Smells of forest and greenery enveloped her instantly. She was frozen for a moment, drinking in the scene. The ax slipped from her fingers as she gasped. It clanked to the floor like a broken dream.

Could it be? Was this where it would end?

The other four princesses rushed up behind Snow, each of them sputtering in disbelief at what lie beyond the door.

There, in the center of the massive room, stood the thickest, tallest, most luscious, fruit-bearing giant beanstalk Snow had ever seen. She stared at it, willing her eyes to stay focused, her mind to remain alert. But her efforts were futile. She could feel her consciousness draining. She struggled to speak, but managed only two faint words.

"Find Jack."

Her knees buckled and she slumped to the floor, the screams of the other princesses sounding far, far away. The walls closed in around her and everything darkened. As Snow drifted off, she imagined the most precious thing in all the world.

Her one true love.

READ on for a sneak peek of THE BITCHES OF ENCHANTMENT, book 2 in the Everafter series. Available NOW!

BOOK 2 - SNEAK PEEK

THE BITCHES OF ENCHANTMENT

When last we left our fierce princesses--rulers of the United Kingdoms of Enchantment, they had found themselves in grave peril, facing an unseen enemy, an unknown nemesis. Dare I say, a villain. Not one of mine, of course. No, whoever was behind the spell that stole the memories of my princesses was far darker than any my imagination had ever conceived. This villain--*villains?*--was more cruel than a stepmother, more heartless than a greedy queen, more diabolically patient than a wicked witch. Whoever had cast the spell had a sinister power the likes of which I had never seen in my homeland.

But if you live long enough, as I have, you hear whispers on the wind of such darkness. Of soulless creatures who will stop at nothing to destroy anything--or anyone--who blocks their crooked path. Many have written of them. They exist in the shadows until some thread of their own story unravels, and they seek out a new narrative to inhabit and pollute.

Had I known who was behind the undoing of my heroines, I would have given them the tools to fight the evil. I would have written them their happy endings. Alas, I know not what will become of them now in their strange new world. I know only that together they are more powerful than they ever realized. And that the one destined to save them all need only remain steadfast and strong to rise to victory. Then maybe--just maybe--this won't be the end of their tale.

But the powerful clap of hoof beats, the drumming of soldiers approaching, and the smell of treachery in the air surrounding my tiny cottage as I write this, tells me that it could be the end of mine.

~Jacob Grimm
　　The Scribe

ONE - Jack

This was Jack Bean's first kidnapping and he wasn't quite sure of the protocol. "Excuse me, Bella? Would you mind cracking a window, please? It's a bit stuffy back here."

Jack was lying prone on the back seat of a long car, his hands and feet bound. He wasn't sure why the two crazy women who had abducted him from his home in the middle of the night hadn't taped his mouth shut too, but he was grateful for that. He was still wearing his pajamas and slippers, and he felt that if he had been stripped of one last dignity, it would have broken him. As it was, he would have to quit his job as psychologist of the damned (a title he had only thought of as he was being hog-tied by a skinny brunette with sharp boots, screaming, "You had to make it difficult, didn't you!") and move to another country. Maybe an island. Where the only women were kindly nurturers who wore shapeless dresses, carried a baby on each hip and always had soup on the stove.

In the front seat, Aura sighed. "Look, Doc, we tried to

reason with you. We tried to explain things, but this is one of those, 'you have to see it to believe it' kind of scenarios."

A cool breeze blew through the car and Jack smelled the kind of artificial vanilla scent that came from those cardboard trees people hung on their rearview mirrors.

Jack said, "No matter what the problem, kidnapping is never the answer, Aura. You've been doing so well in your group sessions. You've made so much progress. How could you throw it all away? You realize, of course, that I'll have to report this. Both of you are going to be right back in front of the judge tomorrow."

Jack wondered how he could have failed so miserably. Where had he gone wrong? He knew the group from Granny's Home for Girls were challenging. Hell, they were criminals, not members of polite society. But *this*? This he never saw coming. And to top it all off he really had to relieve himself. He'd been about to do just that when Aura had broken into his house. He didn't know how she had picked the lock, slid the chain off the door, cracked the security code, and hacked the two deadbolts, but she'd done it with stealth and efficiency. He hadn't even heard her and Bella slip through the door.

"Fuck the judge," Bella said like she was giving a combat order.

Aura said, "You think she has something to do with it?"

Bella said, "I'd bet my Beast on it."

Jack had no idea what they were talking about. All he knew was that after they had barged into his home, they rambled on about some kind of curse and that they needed Jack's help, something about magic, and would he just come with them and they'd explain it on the way.

It was nonsense. Gibberish. He had asked them if they had gotten into their housemate Cindy's tequila stash. (Cindy was still a work in progress, but Jack felt he was making headway with her.) Apparently, that had been the wrong thing to say because two seconds later, Bella swept his legs out from under him and was flipping him over while Aura handed her a rope.

Women. Sometimes they were nothing but trouble.

Except one. The one Jack couldn't get out of his mind from the moment he'd laid eyes on her. Skin like rich cream, hair the shade of a starry night, lips the color of red velvet.

Snow White. His heart beat faster just thinking about her.

And now, thanks to these two bitches, he would probably never see her again.

Jack kicked the back of the driver's seat. Aura grunted, and he wasn't ashamed that the sound of her pain brought him a hint of satisfaction.

"Do that again and you'll be able to hit those high notes at choir practice," Aura growled.

"Be nice," Bella said. "Think of Snow."

At the sound of that sweet angel's name, Jack perked up. Then he got angry.

"All right, ladies that's it. I demand you tell me what is going on right this instant." Jack thought his voice sounded authoritative.

"You're not in a position to demand anything, Doc. In fact, you're kind of in a position to be roasted over an open pit, so don't push it," Aura said.

Jack heard a thump and Aura yelped. "Goddammit, Bella, that hurt. Jeez, doesn't anyone know it's a bad idea to kick and punch the person driving the car? I'm going eighty miles an hour, for fuck's sake."

Bella ignored Aura, tipped her head over the seat back and said, "Jack, just hold tight. We're almost there. Then we'll explain everything."

Almost where? Jack thought. Then he kicked Aura's seat again, knowing it was childish and not caring.

Two - Robin

Robin Hood gently laid the unconscious ruler of Enchantment down on a bed unfit for a queen as Beast, the enormous striped dog with the pointy ears and threatening canines, settled in near the doorway, watching him. The makeshift bed was composed of flattened pillows Robin had liberated from the worn, elaborately carved antique furniture in Granny's living room. He had found an intricately stitched quilt in one of the old woman's closets and laid that across Snow White's lifeless body. He moved with ease and care, respect and honor. A soldier laying a flag across a fallen man. Or woman, as it were.

The giant beanstalk that crowded the space was a harsh reminder of Robin's shortcomings. Magic was not his forte and he didn't know how to remedy this situation. He felt helpless, and it tore at him like barbed wire across virgin flesh. He stared at the imposing plant, its oven mitt-sized leaves waving at him. Mocking him. He thought, as he turned back to Snow, that he heard it snicker.

The princess's chest rose every so often, but her eyelids didn't so much as flutter. Robin fluffed a pillow beneath her head. Laid her arms across her chest. Removed her shoes. She looked peaceful, as if asleep--a lie that brought no comfort.

A gray grief washed through Robin. The kind that whispered in your ear the promise of hope, but filled your heart with black smoke. She was dying, he knew. And nothing in his world would ever be the same.

It was Snow who had pardoned Robin for his crimes back in Enchantment. It was Snow who saw that while he broke the law, he was, in his own way, doling out justice. How had she said it in court that day? "You have taken care of my people better than I have, Robin Hood. For that you will not be punished. You will be rewarded." And with those words and the wave of a scepter, he was a free man.

The pale princess didn't see things in black and white like some leaders. She saw them in silver and gold.

He became her soldier, her confidant, her ally. Commander of all the sovereign's men. And now he had failed in his mission to guard her and her castle.

Robin stared down at the fallen queen and wished for so many things.

He wished that his true love, Marion, could be by his side. He wished he had never been married to that wretched woman Red Riding, and he wished, with everything he held holy and dear, that his men were near, ready for battle.

Because Robin knew, in that moment, he was preparing for war.

The former probation officer sighed and straightened. He removed his cowboy hat and studied Snow for several heart-beats. Worry tightened his jawline, and anger festered in his belly like a hissing snake.

There was a hot flash of shame as he recalled how he had once valiantly declared to protect her unconditionally. She and all the other princesses of the sacred land he called home. Robin's lips moved softly, as he repeated that vow now, hand crossed over his heart. "I, Robin Hood, appointed leader of the noble Knights of the Five Crowns, do solemnly swear with the blood of my veins to guard the princesses of the sacred land of Enchantment with my bow, with my courage, and with my very life-force. So be it now, so be it always."

Robin felt a mist in his eyes as he looked down at Snow. He quickly blinked it away and placed a rough, large hand across the heart of his queen.

Then he made a new vow.

One that promised to destroy whomever had wrought this havoc on his kingdom.

One that slowly seeped through his heart and rushed into his veins, turning his blood into a cold, angry river.

One that would, in time, show a side of Robin Hood no one had ever seen before.

The thief-turned-lawman-turned-cowboy leaned down and whispered in Snow White's ear, "Fear not, princess, for I promise you this. There will be hell to pay."

With that, Robin straightened up, placed his hat back on his head, and went to check on his prisoner.

The Bitches of Enchantment, Book 2 of the Everafter Series AVAILABLE NOW!

Thank you for reading! If you enjoyed the book, please consider leaving a review at your favorite site. Reviews help me to bring you more books that you love.

For more magical reading, check out my Stacy Justice *series.*

For important news on upcoming publications, sales and free stories, sign up at www.authorbarbraannino.com. *You can also follow me on social media at* Facebook, Instagram BookBub, *and* Amazon. *You'll always get notified of new releases and great deals if you follow me on* BookBub *and* Amazon.

* There's also a PRIVATE *reader group filled with amazing, supportive people and a whole lot of fun. Feel free to stop by and say hello. Or shoot me an email at* author@ authorbarbraannino.com. *I'd love to hear from you!*

ALSO BY BARBRA ANNINO

The Stacy Justice World

A spellbinding series that dazzles with magic, mystery and mayhem.

Amethyst Witch

Opal Fire

Bloodstone

Tiger's Eye

Emerald Isle

Obsidian Curse

Phantom Quartz (Tisiphone cameo)

Jaded Witch – Coming Soon

A Tale of Three Witches – Novella

Deadly Diamonds – Novella

Witches Be Crazy – Novella

Thor and Peace – Spin-off

Thor Games – Spin-off

Geraghty Girls Recipes – Recipe Companion

The Everafter World

A laugh out loud fairy tale featuring modern-day princesses with attitude.

The Bitches of Everafter

The Bitches of Enchantment

The Bitches of Oz – Coming Soon

Fury Rising (Stacy Justice cameo)

If you like your heroines fierce and your heroes tough and no nonsense then you'll love Tisi and Archer!

ABOUT THE AUTHOR

Barbra Annino lives in North Carolina with her husband and their goofy Great Danes. When she's not writing, she can be found somewhere in nature plotting her next story.

Made in the USA
Las Vegas, NV
29 December 2022